"YOU ARE A REMARKABLE MAN, FARGO . . . TRULY REMARKABLE."

Fargo saw Isabel's eyes search his face. "Forget the Arabians, Fargo. Let us be friends," she said.

"You've a one-track mind," Fargo said.

She shrugged. "It would be best that way," she said. The tear in her blouse had pulled deeper, and her left breast swelled beautifully upward, exposing it almost completely.

"You're a beautiful woman. Let's be lovers," he said.

"You have a one-track mind," Isabel reproached.

He echoed her shrug, pressing his mouth over hers. . . .

𝒪

Exciting Westerns by Jon Sharpe

THE TRAILSMAN 31

SIX-GUN
SOMBREROS

by

Jon Sharpe

A SIGNET BOOK

NEW AMERICAN LIBRARY

NAL BOOKS ARE AVAILABLE AT QUANTITY DISCOUNTS
WHEN USED TO PROMOTE PRODUCTS OR SERVICES.
FOR INFORMATION PLEASE WRITE TO PREMIUM MARKETING DIVISION.
NEW AMERICAN LIBRARY, 1633 BROADWAY,
NEW YORK, NEW YORK 10019.

The first chapter of this book appeared in *White Savage*, the thirtieth volume of this series.

SIGNET TRADEMARK REG. U.S. PAT. OFF. AND FOREIGN COUNTRIES
REGISTERED TRADEMARK—MARCA REGISTRADA
HECHO EN CHICAGO, U.S.A.

SIGNET, SIGNET CLASSIC, MENTOR, PLUME, MERIDIAN and NAL BOOKS are published by New American Library, 1633 Broadway, New York, New York 10019

First Printing, July, 1984

1 2 3 4 5 6 7 8 9

PRINTED IN THE UNITED STATES OF AMERICA

The Trailsman

Beginnings . . . they bend the tree and they mark the man. Skye Fargo was born when he was eighteen. Terror was his midwife, vengeance his first cry. Killing spawned Skye Fargo, ruthless, cold-blooded murder. Out of the acrid smoke of gunpowder still hanging in the air, he rose, cried out a promise never forgotten.

The Trailsman, they began to call him, all across the West: searcher, scout, hunter, the man who could see where others only looked, his skills for hire but not his soul, the man who lived each day to the fullest, yet trailed each tomorrow. Skye Fargo, the Trailsman, the seeker who could take the wildness of a land and the wanting of a woman and make them his own.

*1864, a town called Laredo
but the name really spelled Texas,
Mexico and trouble . . . .*

1

He saw the trouble coming and swore softly under his breath. It began the minute the couple drew up in front of the Dusty Dollar and he watched from his seat by the plate-glass window of the saloon. Skye Fargo took another bite of his roast-beef sandwich and swore silently again. He wasn't in the mood for playing hero, certainly not in this stinking hot, dry-dust town. But the trouble was coming and he knew he couldn't just sit by, not with the girl going to be smack in the middle of it.

Mexicans, Fargo observed, the girl attractive—black hair; very round, deep-brown eyes set wide apart; full red lips; a broad face, earthy, peasant vitality in it. A white, scoop-neck blouse lay over large, billowy breasts. The man with her not much more than a boy, moderately tall but with a slight, narrow build, dark eyebrows and eyes, and a straight nose on a thin face that sported the pencil-thin trademark mustasche. Truth was, Fargo found himself thinking, neither seemed the type to own the rig in which they'd drawn up before the Dusty Dollar. His eyes went to the wagon again, a graceful, fringe-topped surrey, a two-seater with wine sides and yellow wheels. A dark-red velvet carpet, cloth upholstery on the back of the seats, and oil lamps completed the picture of a really beautiful, elegant surrey, a rich man's surrey.

Fargo had watched the young man and the girl step

down from the fancy surrey and enter the saloon, and he'd seen the trouble come in with them—four drifters, three watery-eyed, scroungy desert lizards, one a big, burly character with hard, dark eyes and a face that looked as though it were made of pitted, pockmarked, worn leather. Fargo watched the man's hard eyes devour the girl as the quartet followed her into the saloon. The burly one wore a Walker Colt polished to a high gloss, Fargo noted. The girl and the young man sat down at a table not far from him, Fargo watched, and the quartet of drifters positioned themselves at the bar, the big one's eyes constantly flicking to the girl. One of the dance-hall girls who doubled as waitresses came over to the pair, and the man ordered a tequila for himself, coffee for the girl.

"Someone is meeting us here," Fargo heard the girl inform the waitress and receive a shrug in return, the remark an attempt to explain and placate. A useless attempt, Fargo grunted as the burly one's voice carried clearly from the bar.

"Since when do you let greasers in a decent place?" the man growled at the bartender.

"Their money's as good as anybody's," the bartender said, and shrugged.

"Greasers are greasers," the burly man spit out, swept the saloon with an aggressive glance. It was nearly nightfall and the Dusty Dollar had already started to fill with customers. "Am I right or ain't I?" the man called out.

"You're right," someone agreed from the other side of the saloon, but Fargo saw a few men turn away uncomfortably.

"Jed Cutter's always right," the burly one boomed, and ordered another drink. The three men with him ordered at once, also. Followers, Fargo grunted, but dangerous in their own way—sneaky, mean, the kind

10

that were always cornered rats. "Goddamn greasers," Cutter growled again, and took a long pull on his drink. Fargo watched the fear dance on the girl's face, the man with her trying to hide his with the bravado of a tight jaw and bold glances toward the bar. But the gestures were a cover, nothing more. The way he kept licking his lips and the little nervous motions of his hands told the real story of the churning inside him.

Fargo looked away. Trouble wasn't ready to explode. The burly one hadn't put away enough liquor yet. Fargo's lake-blue eyes had grown hard as blue quartz as he looked out of the window and watched night lower itself over the town. He let his mind turn the events of the day again, none of them calculated to improve his mood. He'd stopped in at the Dusty Dollar for something to eat, a good shot of bourbon, and a little time to think out of the saddle. The message had been waiting for him when he reached Laredo a few short hours back, and his lips thinned as he thought about it. Delays, a five-day delay, and he cursed to himself. He disliked jobs that began wrong, with delays. It was usually a bad omen. There was nothing now but to wait. He wasn't due across the border till morning and there was sure as hell no reason to get there early now.

Fargo sat back, his lips tight with dissatisfaction when the man's voice helped him cut off further musings. "I'm not drinkin' with Mexicans in the place," he heard Cutter say. "You agree, boys?" The three with him snarled instant support and Fargo saw Cutter start for the table with the girl and the young man, his pitted face flushed with liquor. Trouble had arrived, Fargo swore softly.

"Get your greaser asses out of here," Cutter demanded as he neared the table. Fargo saw the young Mexican start to rise to his feet, but the girl's hand dug into his arm.

"No, Felipe," she said.

The young man met Cutter's belligerent face with an attempt at reasonableness that was bound to fail. "We don't want trouble. We wait for someone," he said. "Please leave us alone."

"You telling me what to do, greaser?" Cutter roared. Fargo saw the man's arm shoot out with surprising speed, a short, looping blow that caught the young Mexican on the point of the jaw, lifted him off his feet, and sent him sprawling into a nearby table.

The girl screamed as she leapt to her feet, started to go to Felipe as he lay dazed on the floor. Cutter moved again with unexpected speed, caught her by one arm and swung her in a wide arc, flung her into the grip of his three companions.

"Hold her. We'll take her outside ourselves for a little funnin'." Cutter laughed with crude anticipation in the sound. The shot exploded in the saloon, tore a hole in Cutter's hat only a fraction of an inch from his temple. He turned, surprise and disbelief in his pitted face as he stared at the big man with the Colt in his hand.

Fargo's eyes flicked to the three holding the girl, saw the mean cornered-rat hate in their eyes as they stared back.

"Let her go," he said as the other patrons in the saloon backed to the far end of the room.

Cutter's burly frame straightened, but the frown of surprise stayed on his pockmarked face. "Who the hell are you?" he rasped.

"Little Bo Peep. Let her go," Fargo growled. He saw Cutter eye the big Colt and decide against trying to draw his own gun. But one of the three holding the girl had different ideas, a small, wiry figure with a sharp nose. Fargo saw the man's hand edging toward his holster.

"You got to be crazy, mister," Cutter said. "You can't take all of us. We've got four guns here."

Fargo fired and the small wiry figure did a half backflip, his gun partly out of its holster as the bullet slammed into his middle. "Three," Fargo corrected.

Cutter stared at the wiry form sprawled on the saloon floor, chest turning dark red, brought his gaze back to the big man with the Colt. "Do what the man says. He's got the drop on us," Cutter said to his companions as his eyes stayed on Fargo. They released the girl and she ran to Felipe, who was holding his stomach as he tried to pull himself up.

Fargo moved sideways, kept his gun trained on Cutter, took in the other two with quick split-second glances. Using his left arm, he helped the girl get the young Mexican on his feet, but the man stayed half bent over, one hand holding his stomach.

"Get outside," Fargo said to the girl. He began to back toward the door, watched Cutter's eyes grow dark with anger and frustration. The man desperately wanted to go for his gun, but his sense of survival told him not to try. Fargo, one arm helping to hold Felipe, felt the swinging doors to the saloon at his back, pushed, and they came open and he was outside in the darkness of the night.

He looked down at Felipe, saw the man lift his head. "Gracias, señor, gracias," the young Mexican breathed. "My stomach, it is torn apart."

"Get into your rig and get the hell out of here," Fargo said, boosted Felipe half into the seat.

The girl halted, her round, wide eyes on him. "No, we cannot go. We wait for someone to meet us," she said.

"You'll wait dead if you stay," Fargo barked. "They'll be coming to kill you now."

"And you, too, señor," she said, concern in her wide, sensuous face. "They will come to kill you."

"I don't kill easy," Fargo said. "Now get this rig out of here before it's too late." He saw despair and indecision tear at her, took one hand, and boosted her into the elegant surrey. "Get out of here," he said.

She took the reins, paused to look at him. "The man who comes to see us, he will wear a red bandanna around his neck," she said. "If you see him, tell him what happened, *por favor, señor.*"

Fargo nodded, slapped the horse hard on the rump, and the animal broke into an instant burst of speed. Fargo spun around, backed across the street into the deep shadows of a shuttered storefront. He didn't watch the swinging doors of the saloon. Cutter would know better than to burst out that way. He'd go out the back and come around the sides. Fargo dropped to one knee, the Colt in his hand, waiting, his eyes moving from one side of the saloon to the other. The alleyway on the right showed the first movement, a shadowy shape carefully edging beyond the line of the building. Fargo raised the Colt, waited as the shadowed form still stayed mostly behind the wall.

"You bastard, we know you're out there. You're a dead man, you hear, a dead man," the voice exploded. Not Cutter's booming voice, lighter, with more whine in it.

One of the other two, Fargo grunted, stayed in his crouch. The shadowed shape suddenly moved, became a figure as the man leapt from the alleyway. He came out firing, a gun in each hand, sprayed bullets as he turned, down the street first, then across toward where Fargo crouched. All wild, frenzied shots, yet dangerous and deadly in their sheer numbers. Fargo heard one splinter the wood inches from his head, and his finger tightened on the trigger of the big Colt. He fired once and the figure staggered, groaned, crumpled to the ground, both guns falling from the man's hands.

14

Fargo caught the sound of racing footsteps at the alleyway at the other side of the saloon, whirled, but too late, the figures gone from sight. He cursed softly. Cutter and the second man. A grim sound escaped Fargo's lips. It wasn't hard to see what had happened. They'd told the first one to rush out and blast away from one side while they did the same from the other. But instead they'd used the diversion to make their break. They'd made a sacrifice out of him, and Fargo stared at the still figure in front of the alleyway. Perhaps stupidity deserved nothing better, he thought grimly, dropping to one knee and pressing himself against the shuttered window.

Cutter and the other man were loose in the night, stalking him, and his eyes narrowed as they peered up and down the street, which had been emptied by the gunfire. He stayed motionless. Many buildings had outside stairways that led to the roofs. Cutter could have reached a rooftop, positioned himself with a perfect view of anything that moved below. If so, he had the advantage of a view, but that wouldn't be enough. Cutter was no hunter. He was a gunslinging bully, a vicious drifter, and nothing more. He had neither the learning nor the character to know what it meant to wait as the wild creatures wait, that special brand of patience, the mark of the true hunter that made waiting a part of acting. The other drifter was but a pale copy. They'd destroy their advantage. He estimated perhaps five minutes at the most.

Fargo smiled as his guess proved wrong by three minutes. He heard the footsteps on the roof above him. A murmur of voices drifted into the street from the saloon, but no one came out. They sensed it wasn't over yet. Fargo stayed motionless, listened to the footsteps moving carefully, slowly over the roof. He felt the frown dig hard at him suddenly. One pair of footsteps only. He whirled just as the man leapt from behind the corner of the building, firing fast, a hail of bullets slamming along the front of the shuttered window. Fargo dropped, rolled, felt two shots graze the back of his neck as he continued to roll. He heard the three shots from the rooftop slam into the ground, too close, as he came up against a water trough, crawled under it, drew his long legs in after him as another shot nicked the heel of his boot.

He lay there, heard the sound of his own breathing as the shots halted for a moment. He could see along the street with a kind of worm's-eye view, peered past the end of a porch, followed the rutted tracks of wagon wheels to the corner of the building. He saw the boots, watched as they moved, began to run. The figure was racing across the street to get a better angle at the water trough. Fargo pushed his arm forward, the Colt held steady in one hand, followed the running boots. He paused a second more, saw the boots slow, start to turn, and he fired at the right one. He heard the man's scream of pain first, then saw the man's face come into view as he fell to the ground, one hand clutching his ankle. Fargo fired and the man stopped clutching his ankle as his face blew apart in an explosion of bone, flesh, and blood.

Fargo pulled his hat off, edged it out from beneath the water trough. There was no shot and he pushed himself out from beneath the trough, sent a darting glance at the rooftop. It was empty. He pulled himself to his feet, darted through the space between the building, and ran to the rear, moved out carefully, his eyes sweeping the rooftops to the right and the left. They were all empty. Cutter had come down but not to lie in wait. He'd have stayed on the rooftops for that. He'd come down to run. He'd had enough.

"Damn," Fargo murmured as he raced back between the buildings to the street. Cutter was the kind that would run only far enough to lie in wait somewhere else for a chance to dry-gulch one. Fargo reached the front of the building and his glance snapped to the hitching post in front of the saloon as the burly figure started to send the horse into a gallop.

"Hold it," Fargo shouted.

Cutter whirled the horse, raced straight at him, firing as he came. Fargo leapt to one side, hit the building wall, dropped low as two shots plowed into the wood above his head. He got a shot off with the Colt held low, saw it graze the man's shoulder. He started to raise the Colt, but Cutter was atop him, leaping at him from the saddle. Fargo twisted, took the force of the man's body on his shoulder and arm, yet it was enough to send him sprawling into the building. He bounced off the wall, fell to his knees, and saw Cutter on the ground, retrieving the gun, which had slipped from his grip.

Fargo raised the big Colt, leveled it at the man. "Drop it," he said.

Cutter paused, his fingers just touching the butt of the gun on the ground. His eyes glanced sideways at the big man with the big Colt. He pulled his hand back, straightened up.

"Sure," he said. "No sense trying against the odds."

"No sense," Fargo said. He moved forward, and Cutter backed away from the gun on the ground. Fargo reached down, scooped up the revolver, and pushed it into his belt. He backed to where Cutter's horse had halted and pulled the rifle from the saddle holster, flung it on the ground. "I ought to put a bullet in you," he said to the man. "But I've never been much for shooting an unarmed man. Get on your horse and ride out of here. Keep riding. I see you again and I'll change my mind."

Fargo stepped back and watched Cutter walk to the horse, pull himself sullenly into the saddle. The man sent the horse into a slow walk and Fargo watched him for a moment, finally holstered the Colt, and turned to where his own horse waited. He'd just reached the Ovaro when his mountain-cat hearing caught the soft click of a hammer being pulled back. He dropped, an instant, automatic reaction, and the shot exploded, the bullet skimming the top of his hat. The big Colt .45 was in his hand at once as he whirled, saw Cutter on the horse, halted, the small revolver in his hand. Fargo fired two shots that sounded almost as one. Cutter toppled from the horse slowly, bending forward first, then falling to the ground, as though he were rehearsing the fall. But it was a final performance, a rehearsal only for death. He'd had the small gun inside his shirt, Fargo nodded grimly as he straightened up.

He drew a deep breath, holstered the Colt, and climbed onto the magnificent Ovaro. He walked the horse slowly away, the animal's pure-white midsection and jet-black fore and hind quarters glistening under a pale moon. He wasn't waiting around for someone in a red bandanna to show up. He'd had enough of Laredo for one day, and he steered his way from town into the dry, flat Texas border country, found a cluster of pecan trees, and made camp. He laid out his bedroll, undressed, and stretched out on it. Delays, trouble, bad omens, he grunted. They came in threes. He let his thoughts go back to what had brought him to the Mexican border country. It had begun simply enough: a damn good offer made by an old friend, Bill Alderson, back in Kansas.

"These horses down across the border, Fargo, they're the finest stock I've ever seen," Bill had told him. "The man who's bred them, one of the old first families in Mexico, needs money, and he agreed to sell a good part of his stock to me. Took a lot of persuading on my part. Had to agree to keep to his breeding practices, which I'd want to do anyway." Bill had leaned forward, warming to his story. "Those horses will let me become the leading breeder of fine stock in America, Fargo. There's going to be plenty of call for fine horses out here one day. I could sell anything I raise back East right now for a small fortune."

"And you want me to get these horses back to you in one piece," Fargo said. "No wonder you're pushing out so much money."

"It won't be easy. You're the only man I know with a chance of doing it," Bill had said. "I've paid half the money for the horses already and I'll give you a check for the other half. My cousin, Sam Alderson, is outside Laredo. He's rounding up six of the best wranglers in all Texas for you. He'll have them waiting when you get there."

Fargo let the conversation slide from his thoughts, but that's how it had started: good money, good talk, and a job that held enough difficulties without adding more. But the message that had been waiting for him when he reached Laredo had been from Bill Alderson's cousin. The wranglers he was gathering wouldn't be on hand for another five days. Fargo shook his head in disgust and let his thoughts drift to the attractive, full-busted, brown-eyed girl and the young Mexican, Felipe. Something had brought them to the Dusty Dollars. No casual thing, that was certain. They'd been filled with fear and anxiety. He could let himself imagine a thousand different explanations, speculate endlessly, but he closed off his thoughts. It would remain one more passing incident to wonder about when the nights were long and boring.

He turned on his side and slept, the big Colt resting against his fingertips.

The hot sun woke him and he rose, washed at a tiny

19

rivulet of water that coursed along the dry ground. His eyes swept the land, the town out of sight behind him, the Mexican border in front of him. The great river coursed sluggishly at this point, the physical delineation between the Republic of Texas and the Sovereign State of Mexico. On this side, the river was called the Rio Grande, the great river. The Mexicans called it the Río Bravo del Norte, the brave river of the north. Same river, two names. It was that way with so much here in this borderland that had seen so much enmity. It was as though neither country would use the other's name for anything.

Fargo wanted to complete his business and head out of here as quickly as he could. But he had five days to cool his heels, dammit.

He saddled the Ovaro and turned the horse southward, slowly eased the animal into the warm waters of the broad river. When he emerged, he was in Mexico, a country chock full of its own problems. He headed west, paralleling the great river, following the instructions Bill Alderson had given him. "You'll see it when you reach it. You can't miss it," Bill had told him, and his words proved right as Fargo came upon the carefully tended white fences first, then the low-roofed stone stables and the vast expanse of corrals. The main house rose up palatially with terraced gardens, tile-shingled roofs, a high, beautifully carved wrought-iron gate at the entranceway. The sign hung across one of the two stone arches beside the gate: EL RANCHO DEL ÁRABE, the Ranch of the Arab.

Fargo rode slowly into the grounds of the main house, took in a dozen vaqueros in their flat-brimmed hats and Spanish rigged saddles with the cinch and latigo straps way up in front of the horse's underside. He had just rounded the circular path to the main entrance of the house when he reined up. A two-seater surrey rested near the entrance, wine sides with yellow wheels, upholstered seats, and oil lamps.

2

Fargo stared at the surrey. There'd not be two like it. That would be stretching the long arm of coincidence out of its socket. He slowly rode past the rig, peered at the thin, yellow wheels. Fresh dirt on them, sandy-brown dirt, the kind on the road from Laredo. He halted before the tall door of the main house and pushed aside the surprise that stabbed at him as he dismounted. The door opened just as he turned to it, a man wearing a white houseboy's jacket holding the doorknob.

"Fargo . . . Skye Fargo," the big man with the lake-blue eyes said. "I'm expected."

"Sí, señor," the houseboy said. "I shall tell Don Miguel you are here. Please come in."

He held the door open wider and Fargo stepped through the entrance, cast a glance back at the elegant surrey. "I'll wait if he has company," he said.

"No, señor, that surrey belongs to Don Miguel," the houseboy said. He closed the door and hurried away as Fargo's eyes moved around the grand living room, a magnificent breakfront of dark wood, massive enough not to look lost in the huge room. Chairs were also big, circular, and dark. A long, wine-red settee faced a wall on which family portraits, armor pieces, and crossed swords hung. The other walls held dark-toned tapestries that even the uninitiated could see were priceless pieces.

He saw other rooms opening up from the living room: a long dining hall with a highly polished oak table and an ornate chandelier of cut crystal. It was the kind of house that echoed the name of the man he had come to see . . . Don Miguel Raúl Consaldo-López, a name with the ring and roll of aristocracy and ancient lineage in it.

He turned as the figure entered the room, a tall man wearing a hand-decorated, sleeveless leather vest over an open-necked shirt and dark trousers, white-gray hair, a handsome man with a thin, slightly aquiline nose, a small gray mustasche. He moved with a very straight, autocratic bearing and he had a smile that tried hard not to be condescending and almost succeeded, a man who wore authority as an inherited right. "Señor Fargo," he said, extended his hand. "I am Don Miguel Raúl Consaldo-López. Welcome to Rancho del Árabe."

"Thank you," Fargo said. "Quite a place, from what I've seen."

"Yes, but then the Consaldo-López family came to Mexico with Cortez, with the *conquistadores*." The man smiled. "We have kept the line of our Spanish nobility for centuries, just as I have kept the purity of my Arabian stallions." Fargo saw Don Miguel pause, take in the power of his shoulders and chest with the practiced eye of a man used to appraising conformation and class. "I have the horses ready to go, Fargo," the man said.

Fargo let a little push of air escape his lips. "There'll be a little delay, I'm afraid," he said. "The wranglers I was to pick up won't be here for about a week."

He saw the frown of dismay cross the thin, aristocratic face. "That could cause problems," Don Miguel said. "I'd hoped you would take the horses and be on your way this morning. I also hoped to make quick use of the rest of the money Señor Alderson owes for the horses."

"He gave me a check for that," Fargo said.

23

"Which you are no doubt instructed to hand over when you take the horses," Don Miguel said, and Fargo nodded agreement. The man gave a tiny half-shrug. "And you are wondering now why someone with this house and this ranch would be so concerned with the money," he said.

"Passed through my mind," Fargo admitted.

Don Miguel smiled almost reflectively. "There are many reasons, First, it is a sizable amount, as you know, one any man could use. Second, for the moment, the monthly income to the ranch has all been delayed, even the monies we receive from Europe every two months. You see, I also breed and sell the finest breeding stock in sheep and in cattle and sell them all over the world. The French are very good customers. But money is very tight now in Mexico. This is a land of many problems, Señor Fargo."

"None of it my business," Fargo commented.

"No, of course not," the man said, smiled. "But now that you are here, let me at least show you the horses you will be driving back to Kansas. Please, this way."

Fargo started after the tall, straight figure as Don Miguel moved toward a side door of the house. The girl stepped out from an adjoining room, a basket of wash in her arms. Fargo saw her eyes widen as she saw him, her full lips come open and the billowy breasts lift with the sharp intake of her breath. She wore the same scoop-neck blouse she had on last night and he saw the moment of panic in her eyes, and then she looked away, started to hurry across the room. "Maria," Don Miguel called. "Don't forget to see to the drapes in the master bedroom."

"Sí, señor," the girl said, and Fargo caught the glance she threw at him, silent pleading in it. He said nothing as she disappeared into one of the other rooms, and he followed Don Miguel outside. Once again he pushed aside the little speculations that rose up inside him at once. There were too many possibilities. But the pleading in her eyes had meant that she was hiding something, and he wondered what as Don Miguel led the way toward a stable with a large, circular training ring outside. A short-legged man in chaparajos and a wide-brimmed sombrero came up, a broad, mustached, pleasant face full of deference.

"This is Pedro," Don Miguel introduced. "He is my *gerente*, what you would call your manager." He spoke to the man in tones that carried authority just under the surface pleasantness. "Let the horses out, Pedro. It is time for their run in the ring, anyway."

Fargo watched the man open the stable doors, disappear inside for a moment, and suddenly the cascade of horses burst into the fenced training ring, all running free without halters or bridles. Fargo felt his breath draw in at the absolute beauty of the horses before him, bays and chestnuts, one rare black, grays and whites, each with the arched neck, the dish face, large eyes and small, neat ears, high tail set and the distinctive bulge over the forehead that ran down to just below the eyes that marked the Arabian. Strength, speed, and delicacy of line combined, their breeding evident in every movement as they leapt, cavorted, and ran with the kind of graceful strength only the Arabian possessed. Fargo watched, his eyes alight, though he realized the full worth of his faithful Ovaro, he knew he watched a rare and wonderful collection of steeds.

"Beautiful," he murmured. "Just damn beautiful." His gaze went to Don Miguel and saw the man frowning as he looked out beyond the nearest corral. A lone rider approached at a gallop, drew nearer, and became a young woman with long, jet-black hair blowing in the wind, tresses that shimmered under the sunlight with flashes of black brilliance. She rode a gray Arabian, Fargo saw; she reached the training ring and reined up to a sharp halt and swung from the saddle. He saw a tall young woman: eyes deep, black pools; thin black eyebrows that arched high; a cream-white skin that was somehow tinged with olive; a thin nose in a beautiful, delicately molded face that was nonetheless severely aristocratic. She held herself very straight and her breasts curved upward from deep undersides to push tiny points against the white, silk riding blouse buttoned up to the neck. Narrow hips flowed into long thighs that curved beautifully under the black riding skirt.

"You were not due back till this afternoon," Fargo heard Don Miguel say, a tightness in his voice.

Fargo saw the girl's deep black eyes center on him, undisguised hostility in their blackness. She gave off a strange combination of coldness and sensuality, ice and fire. She didn't take her eyes from him as she answered Don Miguel. "I rode hard. I expected you'd try to be done with it before I returned," she said, anger in her voice. Fargo saw her eyes take in the strength of his chiseled face, the width of his shoulders, the flat hardness of his powerful frame. Her eyes were deep pools of dark hostility and her finely modeled lips almost held cool amusement as she regarded him. He took his eyes from her as the ranch foreman, Pedro, chugged toward them on his short legs.

"Don Miguel," the foreman called. "The merino, she is having trouble with the lamb. Will you come, please?"

"Sí," Don Miguel said, glanced at Fargo. "You will excuse me, please. One of my prize ewes is in whelp." He hurried after the short figure of the ranch manager without waiting for an answer, and Fargo brought his eyes back to the young woman, saw she continued to appraise him. He let his own glance move boldly down her figure, linger on the twin little points that pressed into the blouse as she stood ramrod-straight, returned to the fire-and-ice beauty of her delicately planed face.

"You are the American come for the horses, of course," she said, her English perfect.

He nodded. "Skye Fargo," he said. "You've got a name."

"Isabel," she answered, one thin eyebrow arching faintly.

"Just Isabel?" he said.

The thin, black eyebrows arched a fraction higher. "Isabel Teresa Concepción Consaldo-López. Will that do?" she said. She saw the question form in his eyes and her contained coolness stayed as she answered. "I am Don Miguel's daughter," she said.

He met her unwavering stare, nodded, and turned away; he leaned on the fence, his eyes on the Arabians. The horses had worked off their initial energy and moved smoothly inside the training ring. He watched their magnificence, took in every clean-limbed line. He felt Isabel come to stand beside him, felt her eyes on him.

"Beautiful, aren't they?" she said. "You appreciate them. I can see it in your eyes. At least you have that much in you, even if you know nothing about the Arabian."

He turned to her, his eyes frosting. "You know what the Arabs called their horse?" he growled, and saw the tiny frown touch the smooth olive-cream brow. "They called him *Kehilan*, which is their word for thoroughbred . . . pure. Five thousand years they raised their Arab thoroughbreds, in every part of the Arab countries. When tribes had wars and horses were captured, it was the custom that someone from the losing tribe was allowed to bring the pedigrees of the horses to the winners. That way they could keep the bloodlines going no matter who wound up with the horses." He paused, speared her with a hard stare. "Being smart is one thing. Just thinking you are, is another," he slid at her, turned back to watch the horses, the gesture one of dismissal.

"All right, you know more than most," he heard her say, her voice sharp. "But it will make no difference. You will not take them to Kansas."

He turned to her, his eyes taking in the coldly contained beauty of her. She continued to stand ramrod-straight and the deeply curved breasts pushed hard against the buttoned blouse. "You want to run that past me again," he said.

"You will not take them," she said.

"You've got reasons for that damn-fool remark?" he growled.

Her chin lifted, the black eyes cold fire. "I have reasons," she snapped. "First, the Apache will take them from you. Kill you while they do it."

"They can try," he said.

"Even if you fight off the Apache, I will not see these horses taken to a country where they will be ruined. I won't let that happen," she said.

"Ruined?" He frowned.

"Yes, I know your countrymen. They will breed them just to make money. They will breed them to any common mare. These magnificent horses will be bred down, not up. They will be used to upgrade any peasant mare available so you can sell the foals for more money. They will breed to sell foals only, not to keep the bloodlines pure. I know how you do things in America. I went to school there. I know how you think, how you act, how money is your God."

Fargo watched the fire in the black pits of her beautiful eyes and knew the truth of her words. Most horse breeders getting their hands on these stallions would do exactly as she had so bitterly flung at him. "Bill Alderson's not that kind," he said. "He'll keep the bloodlines, keep the standards as high as you have here."

A tiny snort of derision escaped her lips. "Maybe, but others will offer him money he won't be able to refuse. I can't chance that. I can't and I won't," she said.

"Your pa made a deal, honey. It was his to make, far as I can see. Seems to me you've no say in it," Fargo tossed back.

"He knows how I feel. The horses will not go to your country," she said. The black flame lighted her deep orbs defiantly.

"That a warning?" Fargo asked.

"It is a statement," she returned.

Fargo's eyes narrowed as he faced the tall, slender figure and stared back at her defiant loveliness. "Now, you hear me out, Isabel, honey," he said, his voice cold steel. "Whether you're all right or all wrong about American breeding practices doesn't count a damn. What you want or don't want doesn't mean shit. I've a job to do and I'll do it. I'd hate to see you get in my way."

"That a warning?" she asked coolly, her thin brows arching.

"Statement," he said, and drew a faint smile from her.

"Why would you hate to see me get in your way?" Isabel asked, and he saw the mocking turn at the corners of her finely etched lips.

"Don't like to see anything beautiful get all shot up," he said.

She laughed, a sudden sunburst of brilliance, and threw her head back for an instant. But when she answered, condescension still edged her voice. No doubt it was built-in, he thought. "A compliment, a backhanded one, but still a compliment. How surprising. But then I'd heard you were not a usual man. That is why your Señor Alderson picked you for this."

"You heard right," Fargo said. "You've some time to forget any crazy ideas you had. I'm not pulling out today. There's been a delay."

"Perhaps it will give me time to make you see how wrong and foolish it will be to try and take these horses to Kansas," Isabel said, a trace of smugness in her voice.

"You can try, but I don't convince easy," he said.

"I'll try, and I don't give up easy," she countered, flashing a cool smile suddenly filled with a very female guile.

He shrugged. He wasn't about to tell her that she could give and not win. She'd learn that when the time came. He saw Don Miguel returning, rubbing his hands on a towel.

"It is done," Don Miguel said when he reached them. His eyes moved from his daughter to Fargo. "No doubt Isabel has told you of her feelings," he said.

"We both said our piece," Fargo answered.

"Good. Please feel free to ride the ranch, enjoy yourself here in Mexico, and be my guest for dinner," Don Miguel offered.

"Yes, stay," Isabel said, and made the two words a challenge.

"Why not?" Fargo agreed, his eyes meeting Isabel's black orbs.

"Good. I will go and rest now," she said, turned, and strode to the main house, back held very straight, her hips narrow, a slender rear hardly moving beneath her riding skirt.

"A very spirited young woman, very, how you say, headstrong. She has always been a thorn in my side," Don Miguel said. "My son, Alfredo, is much more reasonable. You will meet him at dinner."

30

Pedro appeared and put the herd of Arabians back into the stable, and Don Miguel walked beside the big man as he returned to the front of the house.

Isabel was there, Fargo saw in surprise, her hands moving over the Ovaro. "A very handsome horse, Fargo. Very *fuerte*, powerful," she said. "An exceptional Ovaro."

"A very special horse." Fargo nodded.

Isabel patted the Ovaro's neck, turned on her heel, and disappeared into the house.

"I must see to other business, Fargo. Till dinner, *hasta luego*," Don Miguel said as he followed his daughter into the house.

Fargo led the Ovaro by the reins, past the training ring, started across the ranch grounds when he glimpsed the white blouse, the girl flattened behind a clay hut. He saw her beckon to him and walked to where she stayed pressed against the wall.

"Thank you, señor, thank you," she breathed. "For not saying anything to Don Miguel."

"María, right?" Fargo said, and the girl nodded, her wide face attractive despite the anxiety in it. "Want to tell me about it?" he asked.

"Not here, not now, only that Felipe is my brother. I heard Don Miguel invite you for dinner. I live here. Can you come when you are through tonight? I will tell you more then," she said.

"I can try. Why are you so afraid?" he asked.

Her deep-brown eyes stayed wide, and he felt the earthy vitality of her again, made more so by her agitation. "Please, come tonight. I will explain more then," she said.

He nodded and she slipped back along the wall, stayed against it as she reached the end of the clay hut and disappeared around the other side. He swung onto the

Ovaro and rode, felt his lips purse in thought. This damn job was rapidly becoming more than picking up a string of horses. One beautiful female full of hostility and her own notions; another warm, earthy one full of anxiety and her own fears. He'd be intrigued if he could shake away the misgivings, and he made a mental note to hunt up Alderson's cousin and see if he couldn't get enough wranglers together for him to ride out.

Fargo turned the Ovaro through the tall, graceful wrought-iron gate, his eyes traveling along the long line of corrals that stretched far beyond the center of the spread. He rode back the way he had come and then turned, paralleled the great river still out of sight as his eyes moved slowly back and forth over the terrain. Most of it flat, but a line of low, rock-bound hills rose to the right on the horizon, sandstone and feldspar mountains, scrub brush, dwarf oak, hackaberry, some slippery elm, rough and rugged hills. He continued to ride slowly, letting the land engrave itself on his mind, making mental notes of the slow rises, short, truncated valleys, a spot that looked from where he rode like a box canyon. He moved closer to the line of rock hills, saw that the base formed a long line of passages and rock canyons before the hills rose sharply.

He turned, continued to scout the land, had let his eyes take in a long line of chaparrals that seemed to stretch all the way to the Río Grande, when he saw the column of riders appear. He halted, watched them come over the low rise of land and wheel toward him, resplendent in green uniforms with gold facings and gold braid on long riding coats over dark-green trousers. He counted fifteen soldiers with an officer in the lead. Each wore a fancy hat with a long, black plume sticking straight up from behind the brim, the officer's hat sporting double rows of gold braid. Fargo's glance took in the sword and carbine each man carried. French light cavalry, Fargo muttered silently as he let the platoon draw up to a halt before him. They rode well-matched dark-brown bays, and the officer moved his horse a few paces nearer.

"Major Andrade, the emperor's *chasseurs à cheval*," he said, his English carrying a fairly heavy French accent. "Your name, *m'sieu?*"

"Fargo, Skye Fargo," the big man said.

The major had a long nose in a long face that seemed pinched and tight under the fancy uniform hat. He did not hide contempt in his eyes, which took in the man on the Ovaro. "American," he bit out.

"That's right," Fargo said softly.

"You have business here in Mexico?" the major asked.

"Maybe. Can't see that's any of your concern," Fargo answered.

The major's pinched face drew irritation into itself. "We are here under the authority of the Mexican government. We have the right to question anyone about anything," he said.

Fargo eyed the troop. They seemed more like toy soldiers in their fancy uniforms than the real thing. But the swords and carbines they carried were real enough. "I've business with Don Miguel Consaldo-López," he said.

"That will be simple enough to verify," the major said. "Meanwhile, we will take your gun."

"Shit you will," Fargo growled as his eyes turned blue quartz.

The French major frowned as he stared at the big man who sat unmoving in the saddle. "I have fourteen *soldats* here," he said.

"I can count," Fargo muttered.

"You are either very stupid or very brave," Major Andrade commented with his brows raised.

33

"Or very quick," Fargo said.

"There is a lot of trouble in Mexico, too many people wandering around with guns. You can pick it up at my headquarters when you are ready to leave Mexico," the major said.

"Forget it," Fargo said.

The major turned to the trooper next to him. "Take this man's gun," he ordered.

Fargo watched the soldier move his horse toward him, but he saw the uncertainty in the man's eyes, his instincts telling him he was in danger. "Call him off or I'll blow that plume right off his hat, for starters," Fargo said.

"*Vantard*," The major spit at him. "Braggart. Take his gun," he barked at the soldier.

The trooper moved his horse forward and Fargo's hand flew to his holster with a motion almost too quick to follow. The big Colt exploded, a single shot, and the tall black plume on the soldier's hat blew off. Fargo saw the man halt, fear leap into his eyes, but Fargo's gaze was riveted on the major. "You like military funerals?" he rasped. "Because you can have one. The next bullet's right between your eyes."

The major stared, astonishment pulling his brows down, and he saw the barrel of the Colt leveled at him. Fear joined the astonishment in his face, and Fargo watched him swallow, compose his pinched countenance. "Your round, *m'sieu*, as I've no wish to have my head blown off. You are obviously a superior marksman," the officer said.

"I try," Fargo answered.

"We shall meet again, I am sure. Next time I shall be more careful not to let you seize the upper hand," the major said.

"You be sure and do that," Fargo growled as the man

34

barked a command to his troops, wheeled his horse, and led his platoon off in a column of twos. Fargo waited until the French disappeared into the distance before he holstered the Colt. Slowly, he turned the Ovaro and went on studying the terrain. It was a deceptive land, this Mexico, hot and dry, almost lifeless, yet it seethed with turmoil. He wanted no part of its strains and stresses. He wanted only to take the horses and leave. He almost felt he'd welcome the problems of the trip back. They'd at least be direct and simple.

He continued to survey the land until the heat of the day gave way to a shimmering purple, and he rode back to the ranch, reached it just as dark wrapped itself around the land.

The houseboy greeted him at the door and showed him to a room where he could clean up. Fargo carried a fresh shirt in from his saddlebag, washed and changed, and felt more presentable when he walked to the huge living room. Don Miguel was there with a young man who had almost the same face except for two things: his hair and brows were black instead of gray and he had the autocratic bearing without the strength. Handsome, with his father's thin nose and finely molded features, the younger man exuded the nervous tension of the weak, a smile just a shade too strained, eyes that moved too quickly.

"My son, Alfredo," Don Miguel introduced. "I have told him about your delay."

"Unfortunate," Alfredo Consaldo-López said. "But do not fear, I don't share my sister's ideas."

Fargo watched Alfredo pour a glass half full of tequila for himself and down half of it in one long pull.

"Alfredo has had an unrewarding day," Don Miguel said, quick to explain his son's obvious tensions. "I sent him to La Brasilia to collect a sizable sum and he was unable to bring back a single *centavo*."

The younger man's face flushed with his sudden explosion of anger. "Everyone's short of money. Everyone's afraid to ship funds. Between the bandoleros and the Juaristas even the French troops cannot guarantee safety," he said, slammed his fist down on the round wooden table.

"I will explain more over dinner," Don Miguel said, and Fargo saw him turn to the doorway, followed his glance to see Isabel enter the room, and he felt his breath suck in at the sheer beauty of her. She halted, clothed in a full-length, form-fitting white silk dress, cut in a deep slit at the neck to reveal both edges of the olive-cream breasts, beautifully tantalizing glimpses. She moved with a gliding, sensuous motion to halt beside the big man with the lake-blue eyes.

"Please," Don Miguel gestured. "This way. Dinner will be ready." He proceeded into the dining room, Alfredo beside him.

Fargo's eyes stayed on Isabel, met the slow smile she offered.

"We have few guests these days. I decided to dress for the occasion," she said.

"Bull, sweetie. You decided to start convincing," he answered.

The black eyes narrowed a fraction. "You are as conceited as you are crude," she returned.

"But I'm right." He smiled cheerfully, fell in beside her as she glided toward the dining room. She cast a sidelong glance at him, a tiny smile touching the corners of her finely etched lips.

"It might be fun convincing you, Fargo," she said.

"Do it right and it will be, even if you lose," he said as he entered the dining room with her.

The long, polished table had been set with a fine lace cloth, tall silver candlesticks, and a bouquet of flowers as a centerpiece. Isabel took a place across from him as Fargo sat down, Don Miguel at the head of the long table. The houseboy served a large platter of spiced beef with yellow rice flavored with jalapeña peppers. Don Miguel poured wineglasses full of a red wine.

"From Argentina, the Mendoza province," he said. "We may have deep disagreements in this house, but we believe in the civilized life at all times, Good wine is one mark of a proper civilization." He smiled, eyed the big man to his right. "I heard you met Major Andrade. He stopped by to ask about you," he said, laughed. "You impressed the major with your marksmanship. But he is not a man to forget things."

"Why do you allow the French in your country?" Fargo asked.

Alfredo answered quickly. "The French are a stabilizing influence. I, and many others, welcome their presence. Without them, the bandoleros and the Juaristas would have the country in chaos."

"The Juaristas?" Fargo prodded.

"Mexico is in a state of turmoil, Señor Fargo," Don Miguel said. "A man named Benito Juárez wants to overthrow the present government and establish what he calls a democratic state. His followers are called the Juaristas."

"Where do you stand?" Fargo queried.

Don Miguel smiled almost sadly. "I support the objectives of Benito Juárez and his Juaristas, of course. I want to see Mexico ruled by Mexicans, not by a foreign country. I only wish Juárez and his followers were of a higher caliber."

"I don't favor Juarez," Alfredo said, and Fargo heard the contempt in his tone. "He and his followers are rabble. The present government is right to ask for French help. Mexico needs stability, not anarchy."

"Mexico needs to get rid of the French," Isabel cut in, her voice sharp. "They want to make Mexico a French colony. There is talk that they look to set up a puppet government and install the Austrian Archduke Maximilian to rule Mexico."

"Those are rumours spread by Juárez," Alfredo snapped. "You are as bad as a peasant fishwife, always spreading wild stories."

"And you, Alfredo, are like a sleepwalker. Your eyes are open but you see nothing," Isabel shot back.

"Please, enough of this in front of our American guest," Don Miguel said.

Isabel threw a quick glance at the big man across from her. "I'm sure Fargo is not bothered one bit. He enjoys a good fight, I'd say," she remarked.

Fargo allowed a slow smile. "Never minded one," he said. He paused, chose his words. "That elegant surrey of yours," he slid out. "I thought I saw it in Laredo last night."

Don Miguel's smile held a trace of grimness. "You may have. It was there," he said. Fargo let his eyes widen in surprise. "I will explain. First, the Juaristas are in trouble," Don Miguel said. "They need money to finance their movement and to buy arms, but the French troops have been able to intercept almost every shipment of funds and gold. The Juaristas must try to reach the next shipment before the French can intercept it. I received word that an informant would tell me how and when the next shipment of gold would come in."

"Why you?" Fargo put in.

"Because it is known that I support the Juárez movement and I have contacts to transmit the information," Don Miguel said. "But there was a condition. The information would only be given to me or to a member of my family. They would trust no one else. Naturally, I felt I would be too easily recognized by French informants, so it was a question of sending my son, my daughter, or both. But I could not risk that. It could have been a trap to kill me or my family. This is a land made of such killings nowadays."

"So you sent someone else," Fargo said.

"Yes, a young woman and her brother. They work for me. I had them go in my surrey, which is well-known on both sides of the border in this region. They went as my daughter and son to meet with the informant."

"And if it was a trap, they'd pay the price, not Alfredo or Isabel," Fargo finished.

Don Miguel shrugged. "The heirs of the Consaldo-López family are much more important to Mexico than two peasants," he said, and turned his palms upward. But it was the apology of those with the right to make decisions with other people's lives.

Fargo drained his wineglass and kept his face bland as he wondered if the man knew what he had really said. Probably not, Fargo murmured inwardly.

Isabel's voice cut into his thoughts and he tucked his conclusions into a corner of his mind. "I wouldn't have let you send María in my place had I been here," he heard her say to her father, her voice sharp.

"The decision was not yours to make," Don Miguel said with equal sharpness, turned to Fargo, and managed a thin smile. "As it turned out, the informant never appeared, it seems, so it all came to nothing."

"It was still wrong, terribly wrong," Isabel repeated angrily.

Alfredo answered, weary condescension in his voice. "It is easy to be righteous when it is safely over. It is a talent of Isabel's," he said.

"Better than a talent for weakness," Isabel flung back with acid on each word, and Fargo saw Alfredo's glare stab at her.

"I'd best be moving on," Fargo said, rising to his feet. "Thank you for a fine meal."

"We have many guest rooms, Fargo. Spend the night and you can return in the morning. Mexico is a dangerous land at night at these times, especially for the foreigner," Don Miguel said.

Fargo let himself seem to wrestle with the thought, though it appealed at once. It would make a visit to María easier. He half-shrugged. "Might be a good idea at that," he allowed. "Much obliged."

"I'll show Fargo to the north guest room," Isabel said quickly, her voice tight.

Don Miguel nodded. "Good, I've some business matters to go over with Alfredo. *Buenas noches,* Señor Fargo," he said, and turned away.

Fargo fell into step beside Isabel's tall, sinuous shape, and she walked beside him in silence, down a corridor hung with old tapestries. He felt the simmering inside her as she opened the door to a room, turned up a lamp, and he saw a large, comfortably furnished room with an oak four-poster bed taking up most of it. Her eyes were narrowed as she turned to him.

"You don't believe what I said, do you?" she thrust at him. "About not allowing María to go in my place."

Fargo shrugged. "No reason not to believe you," he said.

"And no reason to believe me, either," she snapped. His shrug conceded her words. "My brother was just being nasty. He enjoys that," she said.

"Does what I think make that much difference?" Fargo asked, half-smiled.

"Yes," she said.

40

"Why?" he questioned.

"I've just never liked being disbelieved," Isabel answered.

"Probably, but that's not why now," he said, and laughed at her, saw the black eyes flash. "You can't convince someone who doesn't believe you mean what you say," he added.

This time her shrug was concession. "Perhaps," she allowed.

"I'll give you this one," he said. "I'll take your word on it."

"Thank you," she said.

He reached out, curled one hand under her face, felt smooth, firm skin along the delicate line of her jaw. She started to back away but too late as his mouth pressed over the finely etched lips, held there just long enough for the warmth to penetrate her mouth, and then he drew back. The black eyes peered severely at him.

"That was not at all necessary," Isabel said.

"Necessary's one thing. Nice is another," he said.

"Good night, Fargo," she said, making the three words into a rebuke.

He laughed softly as she stepped into the hall. He watched her glide away, hips hardly moving yet her tall figure gliding with smooth sensuousness. "Nice," he said again.

She continued on, not looking back, and he closed the door and stretched out on the bed. He lay still, waited a reasonable time, and when he pushed himself to his feet, he opened the door silently, saw the corridor was dark, the house still, lamps turned off except for one small light near the front door. On steps silent as a bobcat on the prowl he moved down the corridor and slipped out the front door, closing it carefully behind him. Outside, the night was dry and warm, and he stepped quickly across

41

the ground to the little clay hut where a sliver of light slid from a lone, shuttered window. He knocked softly and the door was opened at once, just wide enough to allow him to slip sideways into the hut. He saw a single room, a stone oven and grill at one side, a bed and two small wood chairs. Clothes hung from a thin wooden rod across one side of the room.

"Thank you for coming, *señor*," María said. She had changed out of the scoop-neck blouse into something that looked like a nightdress with a string holding it together at the neck, the rest of the sand-colored fabric billowing loosely to the floor.

He drew on the scant Spanish he knew. "*Me llamo* Skye Fargo," he told her.

María's deep-brown wide eyes moved appreciatively over him. "Skye Fargo," she echoed softly, approvingly. "It has the right *sonido* for you."

"I know why you were in Laredo. Don Miguel explained that to me," Fargo told her, and saw her eyes grow large with instant apprehension.

"You told him what happened?" she breathed.

"No, I didn't," Fargo said. "Calm down. I just got him to talk." He saw the fear slip from her face and she drew a deep sigh of relief. The full, pillowy breasts pushed against the loose nightdress, and the little knot on the string at her neck grew taut. "I came back here to find out why you're so afraid to tell him what happened in Laredo."

María's attractive, wide face grew almost pensive for an instant. "Don Miguel would be angry, very angry, if he knew we ran. He would not understand. He would expect us to stay, no matter what," she said.

"Even if you and Felipe were killed by staying?" Fargo frowned.

María shrugged. "He would understand only that we

ran and that we did not get the message he wanted. He would say we said the wrong things or did the wrong things."

"No, those four bastards were out for trouble. Nothing you said would have turned them off," Fargo answered.

She shrugged again. "He would not believe that. When Don Miguel gives orders, he expects them to be carried out."

"I still want to know why you're so afraid he might find out," Fargo pressed.

"He would turn us out, both of us. Felipe works in the stables here," María said.

"I'm sure you could find other work," Fargo said.

"There is no other work. There is no place else to work, except for another of the big landowners, and they would not hire us if Don Miguel turns us out. They work together that way. That is how they see to it that families stay and work for one ranch for lifetimes—father, sons, and their sons. The little people are not free to go anywhere else," María said.

Fargo turned her words in his mind. Not slavery as the States knew it, but it came out the same way. A different face for the same body.

María's voice intruded on his thoughts. "That is why the people support Benito Juárez. He has promised not only to throw the French out but to make Mexico a country for all the people, not just the rich," she said.

Her words hung inside him, interesting for more reasons than she knew. "You think Juárez has a chance?" he asked.

"It will be difficult," she said. "But I did not ask you here to talk this politics. I do not know about these things. But I know you saved Felipe and me, and said nothing to Don Miguel. I must thank you for these things."

"Forget it," Fargo said.

"No, we do not forget such things, especially a *norteamericano* helping two Mexicans," María said, took a step closer to him. "You were *magnífico* last night, Fargo. Words do not say thank you enough." Her hands came up, pressed against his chest, and he felt her fingers curl. Her full, ruby lips lifted to his, very pliant, moist. They lingered, opened a fraction wider, then pulled back. He peered into the deep-brown eyes, no cool, contained probing there, only a warm softness.

His smile held wryness in it. "Look, María, I'm not one to turn down pleasure but you don't have to be doing this," Fargo said.

"It is not just to thank you. Last night, when I watched you, I said to myself, Never have I seen such an *hombre hermoso*; this is not someone to just let pass by. But I did not think I would ever see you again and suddenly you are here, at the ranch. So it is more than what you think," María told him.

"Good. Wanting's always better than thanking," he said.

"*Sí, querer,*" she murmured. "I know this, I know." The full lips lifted again, pressed against his mouth, and her arms slid around his neck. He felt the tip of her tongue on his lips, a slow, gliding touch. His hands lifted, undid the gun belt, let it slide to the floor as his mouth stayed on hers.

He put a finger under the knot of the drawstring at her neck, pulled, and the loose nightdress fell open, slid from her shoulders, then fell to her waist. He watched the deep, round breasts seem to tumble outward, away, press into him, all warm, pillowy softness. She pulled away, fell back onto the bed, wriggled, and the loose nightdress fell free of her completely.

Fargo stood over her and knew she watched him feast

his eyes on the large breasts, very round, very soft twin circles of the deepest pink with surprisingly small tips in the center of each. He let his eyes move down across the convexity of her belly, a provocatively round little mound, down to the very bushy black triangle, itself a lush luxuriant growth, and thighs full of youth and womanliness combined. He took in a lusty, earthy beauty, a body a little compact, perhaps a little too full everywhere yet bursting with ripeness.

María reached arms upward, beckoned, and he flung clothes off to fall atop her.

Her body seemed on fire, hot to the touch of his skin, and he buried his face into the heavy, pillowed breasts. "Aaaah . . . ah, *sí, sí*, ah, Fargo," María breathed as he rubbed his lips over the deep pink circles, took one, then the other little tip into his mouth, pulled on each, and felt each lengthen under his tongue. "Ah . . . ah, ah, good, so good, *bueno, bueno*," she said, mixing Spanish and English in little gasps. His hand moved slowly over the roundness of her little belly, caressed, and he felt her arms tightening around his neck as her body throbbed under his touch. The rounded curve of her belly held its own earthy sensuousness, softly fleshy, symbol of all the earthy passion that was part of her. He felt her hips lift, push up against his hand as he moved his fingers through the luxuriant thickness of her black nap, the full Venus mound rising under the soft-wire hairs as a tuft of earth rises under wavy broom moss.

He let his hand rub back and forth through the thick black nap and saw her full-fleshed thighs come open, draw up, close, open again. "*Por favor*, Fargo . . . oh, *por favor*," María murmured, and pushed the little mound upward under his hand. He let his finger curl down over the lower edge of her pubic mound, touch the opened, lubricious lips. "Uuuuuaaaah . . . uuuuuuaaaah," the sound came, a low, moaning groan heavy with pleasure.

He moved his finger across the glabrous folds, felt their warm wetness meet his touch. "Fargo, Fargo, oh, oh, oh, oh," María gasped, each sound a short, hard rush of air. "Oh . . . oh, yes, *sí* . . . *sí* . . . oh." He felt her nails digging into the small of his back. "Take me . . . take me, Fargo . . . ah . . . aaaah . . . take me," she muttered, moved one full thigh, curled it around his buttocks, and pulled him to her.

He let his swollen, pulsating organ rest against her luxuriant nap and felt María's legs working to draw him into her. A soft groaning sounded from someplace deep inside her, and her pelvis rose, rotated, beckoned, pressed upward and forward, seeking his gift. "Please, *por favor*, please, Fargo." The words came between the deep groans as she continued to move her hips, the dark, wet welcome open for him, seeking, searching.

He moved, touched her warm, eager lips with the very tip of his throbbing maleness. "Aaaiiieeee . . ." María cried out, a sharp scream. "*Sí, sí* . . . yes, yes . . . oh, Fargo, *sí*," she said, pushed upward to meet him. He drove into her and felt her thighs clasp around him, lowered his face onto the soft, jiggling little belly as she half-rose, her arms around his waist, pushing against him.

María cried out with each of his thrusts and with each of her own answering pushes, her full-fleshed, compact body a throbbing mound of ecstasy. He heard the laugh come from her, a deep sound that surprised him, pure, unvarnished joy.

"Oh, *qué maravilloso*, Fargo . . . *qué maravilloso*," she murmured as her back arched and she shuddered, the pillowy breasts jiggling, and he felt her hands dig into him with renewed strength. "Ah, ah, ah . . . aaaiiiiiiiii," María screamed, the sound bouncing from the clay walls,

and he pressed his face over one full breast. "Aaaaaiiiiiiii
. . ." she screamed again, and he felt her wetness flowing
around him as she exploded in all her lusty, earthy
energy.

She stayed pressed upward as her stomach sucked in
and out, and the low, groaning sounds came from her,
groans yet filled with pleasure, and when finally she fell
back onto the bed, he heard the small laugh come again,
the pure, unvarnished joy inside her—direct, simple,
totally honest.

He fell down half atop her, lay with her as she continued to keep him inside her, thighs still closed around
him. Her hands moved caressingly up and down his
back, and he saw the deep-brown eyes peering at him.
"So good, so good," María said. "But I knew it would be.
From the first moment I saw you I knew it would be that
way with an *hombre* like you." She lay back and he felt
himself slip from her, and gave a tiny gasp that became a
soft murmur of pleasure as he buried his face into the
deep, pillowy breasts, caressed each with his lips, his
tongue, drew each into his mouth, filling, satisfying,
gorging on the warm flesh.

"Sí, sí, again, Fargo, again?" María breathed.

His answer was given by the already rising organ that
he slid forward into the waiting wet warmth as she
opened her legs, and the full-fleshed thighs clasped
around him instantly. But it was not simply her soft flesh
that surrounded, demanded, invited, but the total earth-
iness of her that enveloped, the spirit embracing before
the flesh. María responded with the total, pure pleasure
that she had before, the sounds from her half-laughter,
half-passion, yet both part of the same lusty enjoyment.
When her curved little belly began to suck in and push
upward in quick, hurried motions once again, and her
scream flailed the clay walls, he felt his own ecstasy, that

exploding moment and after, the sudden draining of spirit and flesh—more than usual this time, for with María he had ridden hard and long, giving all she asked for, matching the pure wanting that was part of her pleasure.

She lay beside him finally, on her side, one large full breast half over his chest, and she stroked his face with one tender hand, pushed his black hair back from his forehead. "*Magnífico*," she breathed softly. "You will come back again, Fargo?"

"I'll sure as hell try," Fargo said.

"Good, good," María murmured as she lay back and he enjoyed the full ripeness of her body. Even lying quietly, she exuded an earthy lushness that was its own kind of beauty.

"I'd best be getting back to the main house," he said. "It'll be dawn soon."

"You are leaving in the morning?" María asked.

"For a spell," he said. "Got to see somebody about getting these Arabians out of here."

"Be careful, Fargo. These are dangerous times. There is much trouble everywhere, bandoleros, the French, government soldiers, and the Juaristas. They can all be dangerous," she said.

"I've met the French." He grimaced.

"If you have trouble with Álvarez, tell him you know María at Don Miguel's," she said.

"Who's Álvarez?" Fargo asked.

"He heads the Juaristas in this part of Mexico. He is a rough man, suspicious of everything and everyone. Some say he is a bad man, but he believes in Benito Juárez and he would do anything for the cause. My cousin, Sánchez, is one of his men," María said. "If you meet with Álvarez, remember these things I have told you."

48

"I will," Fargo said as he pushed himself from beside María and began to dress.

"When will you leave with Don Miguel's Arabians?" María asked as he put his gun belt on; he started to answer, stopped himself. He'd no reason to distrust María and he saw no guile in her directness, but she could repeat his words to others, the wrong others. The rules of the country seemed to be to live in tension and distrust, and he decided to play by the rules—for the moment, anyway.

"Can't say for sure yet. Soon as I get enough hands together," he told her, let his eyes move over her earthy, full beauty once again. "I'll find a way to stop back before that day comes," he said.

She nodded happily as she rose, pressed herself against him. "I will wish hard for that," she murmured.

He cupped the voluminous softness of one breast, more than his hand could hold. "That's as good as anything I can think of to wish for." He laughed, pressed his mouth on hers, and felt her instant response. When he pulled away, he left the little clay house quickly, the dawn already tinting the sky pink as he hurried back to the main house and slipped inside. He was pulling off clothes as he entered the guest room, flung himself onto the bed, and let himself get in a few hours' hard sleep.

It was full morning when Fargo rose. He found a large porcelain pitcher of water in a corner of the room. He washed and dressed and had just finished when he peered out the window to see the elegant surrey moving out of the ranch grounds, Alfredo driving, Don Miguel sitting beside him. Fargo watched the surrey go out of sight, turned from the window, and left the room.

The houseboy appeared as he reached the end of the corridor. "Coffee is waiting, *señor*," he said, and gestured to the living room.

Fargo nodded, entered the room to find more than coffee waiting as he saw Isabel, a tailored orange blouse pulled tight over her breasts, a vibrant contrast to the jet hair that hung loose around her shoulders. She fairly shimmered with the orange beauty of a mound cactus flower.

But he caught the anger in her black eyes, watched her glance away as she sipped her coffee. He turned to the tray on the table with the coffeepot and a half-dozen fine china cups and poured a cup of the steaming brew. He took a long, slow sip. "Good coffee," he remarked, and watched Isabel try to fight down the anger inside her, finally lose as her eyes speared him.

"How long have you known María, Fargo?" she tossed at him. "And don't bother to deny you were with her last night. I saw you leave at dawn."

"Insomnia or plain nosiness?" Fargo asked.

"Neither. I often wake early. I like to watch the dawn come up. Then I go back to sleep," Isabel said. "Now answer my question, dammit."

Fargo took a long, slow sip of his coffee to give his racing thoughts time to settle into place. One thing was certain: María feared the results of Don Miguel's wrath more than anything. Protecting Felipe and herself was all important to her. She'd trade reputation for safety anytime, and he'd go with her wishes, he decided. "Can't see that it's any of your business, honey," he answered casually.

The black eyes flared. "Anything that happens on this ranch is my business, especially with a man come to take away the Arabians. Now, how long have you know María? How did you meet her?" she pressed.

"Never met her before last night," Fargo said. "Couldn't sleep, so I went outside. She was there. We got to talking and she invited me in." He smiled tolerantly, chidingly. "Now, how in hell would I know María before that?" he said.

He watched Isabel's eyes narrow in thought and saw her finely etched lips purse. "It is unlikely, I'll admit. I can't imagine how you could have known her," she conceded.

"Now you're using common sense." Fargo smiled affably.

"But you obviously know her now," Isabel speared, waspishness in each word.

"You just fishing or being jealous?" Fargo smiled.

The black eyes blazed at once. "Jealous?" she echoed. "Your conceit is astonishing."

"Comes from being right most times," he said blandly.

"Well, this will be one of the other times," she sniffed.

"Maybe," he allowed, set his cup down, and started for the door. "Thanks for the coffee," he said, saw Isabel put her own cup down and follow him outside to where the Ovaro waited.

"Where are you going now?" she asked.

"To try and get this show on the road," he said as he adjusted the cheek strap on the horse.

"Will you be back today?" she asked.

"Hadn't planned on it," he answered.

"You're not giving me any time to convince you not to try and take the horses," Isabel protested. "That's not fair. You agreed to let me try."

He met her eyes with amusement. "So I did," he said. "All right, I'll stop back later. I'm not one to stop a lady from trying."

He climbed onto the Ovaro as Isabel's eyes narrowed a fraction. He put the horse into a trot and cast a glance back at her tall loveliness, her carriage every bit as elegantly proud as the Arabians she and her father bred. He turned the Ovaro north toward the Rio Grande, Isabel

51

idling in his thoughts. How far would she go to convince him not to take the Arabians? He smiled at the thought. It was almost worth waiting around to find out. Almost, he grunted. But almost wasn't enough. He wanted out of Mexico as fast as he could. The land was a dry whirlpool ready to suck a man in.

He turned off thoughts as the river came into sight and he halted at the bank. The water was a light brown, heavy with silt and mud. The river narrowed in front of him, but the water gathered power and speed to funnel through the spot. He chose a place downriver, wider but calmer, and let the horse cross the river at his own pace.

Bill Alderson's cousin had a spread east of Laredo, he'd been told, and he headed the horse east of town as he emerged onto the soil of the Sovereign State of Texas. He rode with a grimness carried over from the other side of the river.

3

Fargo sat across from the two men on the porch of the simple frame house, a roof overhang holding back the hot sun. Bill Alderson's cousin was very much like him, he noted, same spare frame, same brown-gray hair, and the same way of using words with succinct logic. "Sure I can round you up some local hands," Sam Alderson said. "Won't be worth a damn to you, though. You'll need the very best crew to get those horses to Kansas and that's what I've got coming."

"Meanwhile, I'm waiting on top of some kind of tinderbox," Fargo growled.

Sam Alderson gestured to the man beside him with the short-cropped gray hair and the strong, square face that carried a good two dozen years of wrangling in it. "Tom Bessie, here, is the only one that's showed so far, and you'll be needing a lot more wranglers than Tom," he said. "You'll just have to wait it out till the rest get here."

"I'd feel better with those horses on this side of the border," Fargo said.

Tom Bessie's square face peered at him. "Maybe we could hide them in a box canyon for a few days," he suggested.

"Good idea; only, the two of us couldn't get them there, not those Arabians, especially starting out. They'll be all fire and flames," Fargo said as he rose to his feet.

53

"I'll check back in a day of two. Maybe the others will be here by then. I sure as hell hope so."

"If they get here, they'll be ready and waiting for you," Sam Alderson promised, and Fargo stepped from the porch and climbed onto the Ovaro. He waved at the two men and rode away, headed the horse back toward the Rio Grande. On the Texas side of the river, the ground rose into a series of sandstone ridges and pinnacled rock formations. Fargo rode into one of the lower ridges, surveyed the terrain, marking the breaks in the soft stone that formed exits. He had just reached the end of the ridge when he heard the shots. He spurred the Ovaro up the short but steep side of the ridge and up onto the top. The river lay just below and he saw a lone horseman who had just emerged from the river, and riding hard behind him, the plumed caps and the gold-and-green uniforms of the French *chasseurs*.

Fargo felt the frown dig into his brow. The lone rider had crossed the river to find safety, but the French troops had followed, Major Andrade leading the platoon.

"Bastards," Fargo muttered as he turned his gaze on the fleeing horseman and saw a young boy, perhaps still in his teens, blood streaming from his face and body, his shirt torn to shreds by a whip. Fargo sent the Ovaro along the top of the lowest ridge parallel to the fleeing horseman. The boy rode one of the French horses, undoubtedly stolen from them, barely clinging to the saddle as the *chasseurs* closed in on him.

Fargo spotted a pinnacle of rocks and turned the Ovaro to race up behind them. He swung from the horse and pulled the big Sharps rifle from its saddle holster, scrambled up the rocks to the top, and found a spot that satisfied him. He was just in time to see the French troop catch the boy and pull him from the saddle. He saw Major Andrade dismount, his pinched face drawn even tighter with fury as he strode to the boy on the ground, his riding crop in hand.

"*Chien de voleur,*" the major shouted. "You will talk." He brought the riding crop down across the boy's face and a new stream of blood cascaded from the slash.

Fargo swore as he took aim, slowly tightened his finger against the trigger of the rifle as the major raised the riding crop again. The big Sharps resounded among the rocks as though it were a small cannon, and Fargo heard the major's cry of pain as his hand spouted a little fountain of red and the riding crop flew from his fingers. The major's eyes swiveled up to the pinnacle of rocks as he clutched his hand with a kerchief he whipped from his pocket.

Fargo saw the soldiers peer up along with the major and he lifted his voice. "Let the boy alone," he called.

He saw Major Andrade frown. "*M'sieu* Fargo?" he said.

"You get the cigar," Fargo answered.

"This is none of your affair," the major said, straightening up, fury in his voice. "How dare you shoot me?"

"You're on American soil, mister," Fargo said.

"A simple mistake. It is easy to stray a few hundred yards in error," the major said.

"Not when you have to cross a river. Or didn't you notice your horses were getting their feet wet?" Fargo returned.

He saw the officer glare up at him. "The excitement of the chase." He shrugged. "We will withdraw at once." He barked orders in French and two of the soldiers moved forward to pick up the boy. Fargo's big Sharps barked and the two soldiers jumped back as the dust flew up a fraction of an inch from their feet. "I told you we are withdrawing," Major Andrade shouted angrily.

"Not with him," Fargo said quietly.

"He is our prisoner. He escaped," the major insisted.

"He's on American soil. He stays on it," Fargo said.

"*Imbécile!*" the major shouted, and hissed commands to his soldiers. Fargo saw them swing their carbines up almost in unison as he dropped low behind the rocks. The fusillade of gunshots resounded and little pieces of stone chipped away as the bullets slammed hard into the rock. He kept low, waited another half-dozen seconds as the fusillade died away, then moved quickly, the rifle ready to fire as he poked his head up, blasted two quick shots. Two of the soldiers toppled and the rest began to dive for cover. He fired again and saw a third soldier go down. Major Andrade had dived behind a line of dry shrubbery and Fargo heard his voice shout up at him.

"You cannot hold off my entire platoon, Fargo," the major said.

"Want to bet on that?" Fargo answered. The cover near the river was sparse, most of the soldiers flattened behind small mounds that left them more visible than not. Fargo decided to enforce his words by example and he picked out one soldier, visible from the waist down. He aimed, fired, and the soldier screamed in pain as he twisted to clutch at his shattered knee. "I'll pick off and hold off," Fargo called, "a hell of a lot longer than you can risk." He could almost hear Andrade's teeth gnashing in frustrated fury. The major knew full well what he meant. If a troop of Texas Rangers came by and found the French soldiers on this side of the border, all kinds of hell would break loose. It was a risk the major couldn't afford to take.

"Let us get our wounded," he heard the major call.

"Nobody else," Fargo said harshly, his finger against the trigger of the rifle. He watched the French officer step from his cover as he sighted down the gun barrel, saw him direct his troops to care for the wounded. Fargo

56

waited as they draped the men over their saddles and he saw Major Andrade climb onto his horse.

"I won't forget this, Fargo," the major shouted, and Fargo saw he had wrapped a kerchief over his hand. The man wheeled his horse and set off at a fast canter.

Fargo stayed motionless, watched the French troops cross the river, waited as they reached the other side, kept watching as they rode away from the bank. Only when they were out of sight did he scramble down from the rocks, retrieve the Ovaro, and ride to the end of the ridge and then back to where the lone figure lay on the ground.

Fargo dismounted, knelt down beside the boy, who seemed even younger close at hand. He had been savagely whipped, savagely and systematically, but he was still alive and suddenly the young boy's eyelids fluttered, came open.

"Easy now, they're gone," Fargo said.

The boy's lips moved, tried to form words, but only a hoarse wheeze came from his throat and then the words took shape. "Álvarez . . . tell Álvarez . . . they got nothing . . . nothing . . . tell him," the boy breathed.

"Don't try to talk, and maybe you can tell him yourself," Fargo said as the boy's eyelids fluttered shut again. Fargo looked at the boy's wounds. There was nothing he could do here for him. The whipped, lacerated body needed to be wrapped, the wounds given ointment to soothe and stay the flow of blood. The scars across his face would never completely disappear, Fargo took note angrily. Major Andrade had done a sadistically efficient job, inflicting maximum pain yet keeping the victim alive.

Fargo leaned closer to the boy's face. "Can you hear me?" he asked. The eyelids fluttered in answer. "Just keep breathing. I'll get you someplace safe," Fargo told him. He reached down, picked the limp form up, and laid the boy across the Ovaro's saddle and carefully climbed onto the horse behind the dangling form.

Fargo moved the horse toward the river, and his eyes narrowed as he peered across to the other side. It'd be dangerous once he was across into Mexico. If he had to put the horse into a gallop, it'd just about kill the boy. But he'd die from continued loss of blood if he weren't treated. He eased the Ovaro into the river, took the crossing slow, letting the horse drift with the sluggish current, finally climbed out onto the far bank and was grateful for one thing: the land between the Rio Grande and the Consaldo-López ranch was pretty much flatland, some yucca, a few dwarf trees, low rock forms, nothing that could hide a platoon of soldiers. He'd see them coming long before they spotted him, and he turned the Ovaro south toward the ranch. The boy was still breathing regularly, and still bleeding. Fargo grimaced and brought his gaze down to the ground.

The prints of the French cavalry troop were plain to see, stretched out ahead of him. He followed along the same direction, keeping his eyes on the tracks. He had ridden perhaps another hundred yards and was about to turn southwest when he noticed that two sets of prints moved away from the others. But not sharply, Fargo took note, a slow, sideways movement that paralleled the hoofprints of the rest of the platoon. They seemed to be two riders simply drifting to the side of the others. Most trackers wouldn't have taken them for anything more, but the Trailman's eyes narrowed as he picked up the way the two sets of prints continued to drift away from the others. He followed and saw the two sets of hoofprints suddenly veer off in opposite directions. The tiny smile that touched his mouth was made of hard, tight lines.

Major Andrade was being clever, Fargo grunted silently. The Frenchman was well aware the terrain wouldn't conceal the whole platoon, but there was cover enough for two men to set up an ambush. The ploy would have worked had he not read the drifting prints correctly, Fargo knew.

He slowed the Ovaro and slid from the saddle, began to walk beside the horse, one hand on the Colt at his hip, eyes scanning both sides of the terrain. He was almost within sight of the ranch when he spotted the two small trees, lotewood condalias, each with just enough foliage to hide a man. He had to pass between them or give away the fact that he was waiting and ready. He stayed close to his horse, kept the slow, deliberate pace. His eyes flicked from tree to tree while his head stayed motionless. The soldiers had taken off their caps so the tall plumes wouldn't show, but they'd have to change their plans. He grunted with grim satisfaction. He'd seen to that.

If he'd stayed in the saddle they would have had a clear shot at him without leaving their cover, but walking close beside the Ovaro, he was an impossible target from that distance. They'd have to come charging to get close enough, and that's all he wanted. Once they left their cover, they'd be the clear targets, not him. His hand lifted the Colt from its holster as he neared the two trees, let it dangle at the end of his fingers, close at his side.

The two Frenchmen did exactly as he expected they would: let him pass between before they made their move. His eyes were fastened on the tree nearest to his side of the Ovaro as the horseman burst from the foliage, a flash of gold and green, carbine raised. Fargo dropped to one knee as he pulled the Ovaro to a halt with a tug on the reins, held his fire a second longer as the soldier charged. As the man veered toward him, he fired two shots, and the carbine flipped from the soldier's hands as he pitched forward in the saddle, the gold of his uniform suddenly streaked with red.

Fargo didn't wait to see him fall lifelessly over his mount's neck. Instead, he turned, put his left palm against the Ovaro's underbelly to keep the horse calm, and spun underneath the horse to face the second *chasseur* charging from the other side. He saw the man's eyes search for him, find him, and the soldier pulled back to slow his horse, tried to bring his carbine around. But he was the easy target and the big Colt barked again. The soldier's hands jerked on the reins as the bullet exploded through him. The horse reared, spilled him backward. If the bullet hadn't killed him, the fall did as he landed on his head and Fargo heard the snap of neck vertebrae.

Silence fell on the scene as Fargo ducked out from beneath the Ovaro and raked the horizon with his eyes. There was no sign of Andrade and the rest of the platoon. The major had likely gone on to his camp to wait for his two soldiers to report in with word they had done their job. He was a smug, sadistic bastard, Fargo growled, and he enjoyed thinking about the major's fury when he realized what had happened to his two fancy-uniformed dry-gulchers.

Fargo swung onto the Ovaro, headed the horse on toward the ranch, and when he passed the neat white fences, two *vaqueros*, frowns of curiosity on their faces, swung in close beside him. He saw the elegant surrey outside the main house as he halted, dismounted, and lifted the boy from the saddle, putting him gently on the ground. Others came quickly, stableboys, *vaqueros*, and a few women with clothes baskets who hurried up to stare at the boy's bloody figure.

Fargo knelt down and listened to the boy's breathing. It was harsh but still regular, and he rose as Don Miguel came from the house, Alfredo beside him. The man frowned at the figure on the ground, and Fargo glanced past him to see Isabel hurry out, still in the brilliant orange blouse.

"Who is he?" Don Miguel asked.

Fargo shrugged. "I don't know. I saved him from the French, on the Texas side of the river," he said, and saw María come up, her eyes wide as she stared at the boy.

"I have seen him," María gasped out. "He is one of Álvarez's men."

"He needs bandaging and something for his wounds," Fargo said, and told what had happened in short, terse sentences.

"I'll bring cloths," María said.

"I've some ointment," Isabel added. "Ground walnut bark and yarrow." She hurried into the house, returning just as María brought back an armful of cloth strips. Isabel knelt down beside the boy, began to apply the ointment to his lacerated body while María cleaned away the caked blood and began to bandage the wounds.

"He'll be needing rest and luck if he's going to make it," Fargo said.

"Not here, he can't stay here," Don Miguel said. "You shouldn't have brought him here, Fargo."

"Thought you favored the Juaristas," Fargo said.

Don Miguel continued to stare at the boy with icy disgust. "Being sympathetic is far different from harboring a fugitive," the man said. "I can't have him found here, and the French will come looking, you can be sure. That would destroy my position, my effectiveness in helping the Juaristas."

"Logic but not much sympathy," Fargo commented, drawing a quick glance from Isabel.

"These times require logic, not emotion," Don Miguel said sharply.

Fargo shrugged, the answer perhaps completely correct, but he made no reply.

"He cannot stay here," Alfredo said. "I won't have one of Álvarez's men hiding here. Álvarez is nothing but a *bandolero* and murderer. Like the rest of Juárez's followers, they use the cause as a means of justifying their raiding and killing. To say they are followers of Juárez gives their actions a cloak of respectability. They are all rabble. They will ruin Mexico."

"Finish bandaging him and I'll try to get him back to Álvarez," Fargo said.

"*Imposible!*" Don Miguel said. "No one knows how to reach Álvarez in those rock mountains of his."

"I'll take you. I know part of the way," Fargo heard María say, and he saw Alfredo turn to her, his face an icy sneer.

"Yes, I forgot, you have cousin with that scum of a murderer," Alfredo said.

"I'd appreciate her taking me as far as she can. Maybe Álvarez will find us then," Fargo said.

"If you insist, Fargo." Don Miguel shrugged. "But you don't have to do this. It is none of your affair."

"Got into it. I'll see it through. That's my way," Fargo said.

"Leave him for the French to find and take him back with them," Alfredo snapped. "You're being a fool."

"Been called that before." Fargo smiled slowly, watched María finish securing the bandages that now swathed the boy's body. They had staunched the flow of blood, and under them, Isabel's ointment was no doubt doing its work, also.

"I'll get a horse for María," someone said, and Fargo glanced up to see it was Felipe. He disappeared back toward the stables and Fargo met Alfredo's eyes, anger and condescension in their depths.

"You have made an enemy of Major Andrade. Álvarez won't be your friend. He doesn't know the meaning of the word," the man said.

"Don't give a damn about that," Fargo said calmly.

Felipe returned with a dark-gray gelding and two of the *vaqueros* lifted the boy, placed him over the saddle of the horse.

María climbed onto the horse behind the bandaged form. "I'll ride with him," she said. Fargo nodded agreement. It would leave him free to handle any trouble that might come up. He paused to look at the boy, saw he was in a state of semiconsciousness. He turned to swing onto the Ovaro and found Isabel beside him. "It almost seems you are making reasons not to listen to me," she said.

"Seems I'd make easier ones," he growled, and saw her lips tighten at the reprimand.

"I'll wait," she said.

He nodded, swung the Ovaro in a circle, and followed María as she put the dark-gray gelding into a slow walk. She moved to the rear of the ranch and he saw the low rocks rising on the horizon. He glanced back as the others moved away, all except Isabel. Her tall form stayed, and she watched him ride away with María. She finally turned back to the house as he moved out of sight. He spurred the Ovaro to pull alongside María. "Don Miguel and Alredo had a lot harder words for Álvarez than you did," he remarked.

Her eyes held a hint of defensiveness. "I told you that many think Álvarez is a bad man," she said.

"But you don't," he prodded.

She shrugged. "He is a rough man. All the big land-owners hate him because he has raided their lands, sometimes to take cattle to feed the poor."

"You make him sound like a man of charity," Fargo said.

"No, he is not that," María answered. "But he is not just using Benito Juárez to justify his raiding and killing. Don Miguel is wrong about that. Good or bad, Álvarez believes in Juárez and what he stands for." He saw María's eyes soften as they rested on him. "You have done another brave thing, for the boy this time, standing off the French alone."

"Didn't plan it that way. It just happened," Fargo said. "The same way Isabel knows we were together last night. She saw me leave your place."

María's eyes grew wide, instant apprehension flooding her wide, earthy face. "She suspects about what happened in Laredo?" María breathed.

"No, I made her believe we had just met and you just had to invite me in," Fargo said.

"It is all right," María said quickly, picking up the apology in his voice. "It is better she thinks that than the truth." She flashed a quick, almost sly little smile. "And it is not so very far from the truth," she finished as she turned the dark-gray gelding up a narrow path as they reached the base of the rock mountain formation.

Fargo followed, his eyes scanning the land, the mountain range mostly rock, clay, and sandstone, some basalt. The rock formations rose up in harsh, jagged peaks as though they were the teeth of some giant prehistoric monster. Crevices opened up to run through the rocks, and sudden areas of flat stone expanses opened up unexpectedly.

He missed nothing, made mental notes as María led the way into the rocky fastness. A trio of giant saguaro cactus marked the spot where she took the second pathway upward, and a long line of yucca sprang from tiny crevices where she turned to a third passage. She climbed past a pair of arched boulders that rose as almost identical formations, and he noted the heavy growth of buckthorn where she turned onto still another passage. All the little things that most men would have missed engraved themselves on his mind as he followed María through the narrow space that emerged onto a flat table of rock. He swept the higher peaks and grimaced. They were being watched. He hadn't seen anyone, but he felt the presence of others as the rabbit senses the hawk without seeing it—instinct, that special sense given to those with the wild inside them.

María took a curve that led up and again Fargo scanned the rocks. He saw nothing, but the rock fastness held a thousand crevices. They were not alone, he was certain. The curve led to a higher table of flatland, and as the day began to take on the soft violet of approaching dusk, María halted, glanced at him, and said, "I don't know where we go from here. I've met Sánchez at this spot. I've never gone farther."

Fargo nodded to the far end of the rock plateau. "Let's go on straight," he said, and spurred the Ovaro forward. He had almost crossed the flatland when two single lines of horsemen suddenly filtered out of the rocks on each side of the plateau. They moved slowly, unhurriedly, joined to form a single line that stretched across the table of stone and advanced toward him and María. He let his eyes move across the line of horsemen as they came toward him. Most wore double rows of cartridge belts slung across their chests. All were armed to the teeth with an assortment of handguns, rifles, machetes, and knives. They rode short-legged ponies that were plainly strong but not very fast. He saw young men with tight faces, old men whose years of experience showed in their cynical eyes, and young boys hardly old enough to shave.

The line of horsemen halted in front of him and one man in the center moved his pony a few paces nearer.

"Álvarez," María half-whispered.

Another horseman to the left of the line pushed his pony forward, a younger man with thick, curly black hair. "María," he called out.

"Sánchez," the girl acknowledged.

Fargo's eyes stayed on Álvarez as the man halted, his glance finding the bandaged form across the saddle, returning to the intruders. Fargo saw a wiry figure, an almost gaunt face with a large nose slightly hooked, a thick, drooping black mustache, thin lips, and black eyes that seemed to be pieces of hard coal. It was a face as impassive and uncompromising as the rocks of the mountain fastness, a face that held power and distrust in it, strength and cunning, anger and ruthlessness.

Once again, Álvarez glanced at the boy, and Fargo thought he caught a moment of emotion in the coal-black eyes. The man barked a command and four of the others dismounted, lifted the bandaged figure to the ground, and formed a quick sling for him out of a piece of canvas one produced.

"He lives because of this man," Fargo heard María say, and saw Álvarez fasten his eyes on her. "His name is Fargo. He saved the boy from the French," she went on, switching into rapid Spanish to tell the complete story of what had happened. When she finished, Álvarez brought his eyes back to the big man who sat calmly on the magnificent Ovaro. His eyes appraised and studied with the experience of one who has learned to judge men.

"*Muchas gracias, señor,*" Álvarez said. "Fargo, they call you."

The Trailsman nodded, knew Álvarez searched his face for a sign of nervousness. He would find none, Fargo also knew.

"So you came for the Arabians Don Miguel has sold, and now you are a Juarista," Álvarez said, and Fargo caught the wry humor in the man's voice.

"I'm not anything," Fargo said. "I didn't like the odds and figured he'd had enough done to him already."

"You have helped a Juarista. To the French and their government puppets, that makes you one of us," Álvarez said.

"Don't much care what they think," Fargo said. "What was the boy doing when they caught him?"

"His name is Rafael. He was one of my couriers," the rebel leader said. "Someone must have turned him in. The French pay informants well. What they did to Rafael is nothing to what they have done to others. I have no mercy on them. We must fight as dirty as they do. And we take any help we can."

"Don Miguel told me he supports Benito Juárez," Fargo said.

Álvarez uttered a harsh sound. "Yes, I have heard this," he said.

"You don't believe it," Fargo prodded.

"I believe very few people, and never the wealthy," Álvarez said.

"Perhaps he is a Mexican first and a rich man second," Fargo answered. "Can only the poor have principles, *amigo?*"

"To the rich, principles are an indulgence. To the poor, they are a necessity. But no matter what I believe, Juárez trusts Don Miguel, believes in him," Álvarez said. "He has made use of him as a connection, sometimes for couriers coming in from Texas. But none of it has helped."

"Meaning what?" Fargo questioned.

"The moneys to finance the movement are not getting through. They come in different ways from different places, and always they are intercepted. Somehow, the French or the government troops have information. They get to the shipment before we do."

"The moneys always come the same way?" Fargo asked.

"No, different each time. Sometimes a single courier, sometimes in a wagon, sometimes from the north and down the Mexico side of the border, sometimes straight across from Laredo. It depends how much is coming in and whether it is cash, silver, gold, or bank notes," Álvarez said.

"How do you learn when a shipment is coming?" Fargo questioned.

"Sometimes Juárez channels a message through Don Miguel. Sometimes he sends a courier direct to me. But still the French find out. There is what you *americanos* call a leak."

"Got any suspicions?" Fargo asked, keeping his voice casual. He saw Álvarez's face harden.

"That son of Don Miguel's, that *tacaño*, that no-good, stinking ass. He hates Juárez and the movement. It would be easy for him to listen, overhear, spy. He travels a lot on family business. He could easily make his contacts with the French," Álvarez said, spitting out words. "I have been thinking about killing him for a long time."

"But you haven't," Fargo commented.

"Only out of respect to Benito Juárez, because he still trusts Don Miguel. And, if I am wrong, it would destroy the channel for us. But I am losing patience, *señor*, I tell you that," Álvarez almost shouted, paused, brought his voice under control, and Fargo saw a wily curiosity come into the black eyes. "You ask a lot of questions, Fargo," he said.

"I put a foot in something, I like to know more about it, in case I fall in deeper," Fargo answered casually.

Álvarez laughed suddenly, a hard, tight sound. "And the only reason I have answered you is because of what you did for Rafael," he said.

"Fair enough," Fargo said. "You know, Alfredo doesn't think much of you. He says you are a bandit, that you were always a bandit and nothing more."

"He is right." Álvarez grinned. "But unless you are a wealthy landowner, a bandit is the only way to be a free man in his Mexico. I would rather be a hawk than an ox with a yoke on my shoulders." Álvarez glanced up at the deep dusk moving over the rocks. "You had best leave with María. It will be dark before you are halfway out of these mountains," he said. "Again, *muchas gracias* for what you did for Rafael. *Adiós*, Señor Fargo."

He wheeled his pony abruptly, and Fargo saw him pause for an instant beside María, his eyes peering deep into her, and then he rode on. The others formed a single line behind him, four on foot carrying the canvas with Rafael in it. They disappeared into a passage in the rocks at the end of the flat table of land.

María turned her horse around. "Let us go," she said softly.

Fargo swung in beside her as the dark came over the rocks and he rode slowly, carefully as a half-moon began to lift itself higher into the sky.

"What did you think of Álvarez?" María asked as they rode down one of the passages.

"He may be everything Alfredo says. I have the feeling he is a man who will stop at nothing to get what he wants. But he is no ordinary *bandolero*. He has had good schooling. He knows how to think as well as fight," Fargo answered.

"*Sí*, he was once a student at the University in Chihuahua," María said. "He wanted to be a doctor. But one night two drunken soldiers attacked him. He killed one in the fight. They put him in jail for life. When he finally broke out, years later, he was made of hate."

"How do you know so much about him?" Fargo asked.

"My cousin Sánchez has told me," María answered as they emerged from the passage onto a small circle surrounded by stones. The moon cast a dim light and turned the harsh rocks softer and a warm wind drifted across the little circle. He saw María halt, slide from the horse, and turn to face him. "There will be no one watching to see you leave from here," she said.

"No one at all," he said as he swung to the ground. He unbuckled his bedroll with one hand, tossed it on the ground alongside the deep shadows of the rocks.

María's fingers pulled the buttons on her blouse open and she shook the garment free as she stepped to the bedroll, faced him, and the silver light of the moon bathed the deep, pillowy breasts in its pale glow. She let her skirt fall to the ground, stood naked before him, a silvery earth goddess, the thick, bushy triangle intensely black.

He shed clothes as he moved toward her, fell to his knees on the bedroll when he reached her, and pressed his face deep into the big breasts, let his mouth move from one deep-pink nipple to the other. He felt her arms wrap around his neck, hold his face hard against her.

"Fargo, Fargo, oh, *Dios mío*," she breathed. "I have thought only of you since the other night. It was so *especial*."

"Let's try for two," he murmured, pressed, and she sank back as he kept his face against her breasts. He felt her right arm relax, fall from around his neck as he rubbed his body against the soft fleshiness of her, all smooth cushiony warmth, and then he half-turned, heard the gasp of pleasure as her hand closed around his pulsing hard-soft maleness.

"Oh, *sí, sí* . . . oh, yes . . . oh . . . aaaaah," María breathed as she pressed her fingers around him, caressed, stroked, trembled at the ecstasy of sensation

70

that flowed through her fingers, up into her body, tiny messengers of fire.

He lay back, enjoyed the caressing touch of her as she continued to play, stroke, run her hand up and down his vibrant spear. María pushed her little curved belly against his organ, pressed herself down upon it, and little soft sounds came from her. He felt her half-turn, pull him with her, and he pushed himself up as she fell on her back, slid over her as she continued to hold him with her hand. He felt her guiding him, gently pulling him to her, and her full thighs parted, fell open, and the wiry touch of the bushy nap reached up to press against his pelvis. "Ah . . . ah . . . aaaaaah, Jesús . . . Jesús," María cried out as she pulled him into her, pushed upward to engulf his throbbing eagerness. "Yes, oh, yes, Fargo . . . Fargo . . . aaaaah . . . uuuuooooh," she moaned as he slid deeper inside her, waited, pushed still deeper.

Her low moaning sounds echoed from the circle of rocks that surrounded them, and as he pushed deep, drew back, pushed forward again and again and again, he heard the little gurgle of joy well up from her lips, almost a laugh, the pure pleasure of the body let free, giving all, taking all. His mouth found one deep soft breast and clung to it, surrounded the deep-pink tip as he felt María's soft thighs starting to tighten against him.

Her legs lifted, pressed into his hips, and her moans became quick breathy sounds, quickness increasing, growing louder, more insistent. "Fargo . . . Fargo . . . ah, ah . . . I . . . I . . . *ahora, ahora*." He drew back and rammed deep, let himself explode with her, and her moan became a low scream, a sound harsh with searing ecstasy, almost animallike in its total abandonment. When she fell back against the bedroll, her breath rushed from her in a half-sigh of protest and she held his face into her breasts until her body relaxed, lay still. He drew himself up on one elbow to gaze at her. Her wide mouth formed a smile, pleasured satisfaction in it, and she stretched, rolled on her side, and pressed the little rounded curve of her belly against him. She smiled—a bemused, private little smile—as she glanced up at him.

"What are you thinking about?" he asked.

María rolled onto her back, the smile staying. "About Señorita Isabel," she murmured. "I never thought we would have something in common, but we do now." Fargo waited and her smile widened. "She does not want you to leave with the Arabians. I do not, either," she said.

"You've different reasons." Fargo laughed softly.

"Mine are better," María said, and pulled him to her, wrapped one leg around him, pressed her warm fullness against him.

He lay with her as she half-dozed happily, finally pulled back, and disentangled himself from her. The moon had swung high across the sky, he noted. "We must go," he said. "It'll be damn near dawn when we get back."

She nodded, drew clothes on, and was dressed by the time he had the bedroll back behind his saddle. She rode beside him as he set an easy pace down through the rock mountains. "You are staying at the ranch again?" María asked as they reached the bottom of the rocks and started over the dry soil.

"No," he said. "But I'll stop by in the morning."

She accepted the answer and said nothing more until they reached the rear of the darkened ranch. A faint pink line began to creep along the distant horizon. She leaned over, pressed her lips to his. "I'll be wishing hard again," she murmured, and rode on at once.

He turned the Ovaro, skirted the edges of the ranch, and rode south till he found a chaparral of dwarf trees and bedded down, slept through the dawn sun, and woke when the morning was full, the burning rays quickly turning the dry soil hot. He found a small, clear stream running down a crack in the dry ground, and he washed, refilled his canteen, saw to the Ovaro's needs, and swung into the saddle when he finished shaving.

He felt no need to report to Don Miguel—in fact, the thought rankled, but he'd promised Isabel her chance at convincing him. He'd keep to that much. The possibilities still intrigued him. María had been a most enjoyable surprise, but it'd be nice to see if aristocratic pussy was any different from any other kind.

4

The Arabians were running free in the main corral when he arrived at the ranch; he dismounted, watched the magnificent beauty in motion. He was still leaning against the white fence when Isabel came from the stables leading a striking white Arabian, the horse prancing beside her with pent-up energy, the clean, chiseled head and dark eyes the embodiment of his lineage. Fargo's eyes went to Isabel. She had her onyx hair pulled back severely, and he saw that her face was tight, anger in the black eyes. A cream blouse rested lightly against the tips of her curved breasts, which rose sharply from their deep undersides.

"Let's ride. I don't want to talk here," she said coldly.

"I expected your pa would have questions," Fargo offered.

"He and Alfredo have already talked with María. She told them things went well," Isabel said.

"Hope you didn't wait up," Fargo said blandly, and saw the black eyes narrow at him.

"Hardly," she said. "I've learned you're not one to turn away from anything that comes easy."

"You're sounding jealous again, honey." Fargo laughed.

Her eyes flashed fury. "You keep confusing disgust with jealousy," she snapped.

"Guess so." He grinned.

Isabel spun away, flung herself onto the Arabian, and set off in an angry canter. He caught up to her as she slowed finally, continued to head south, and finally came to a halt in a basin where an underground spring bubbled fitfully but gave off enough water to let the horses cool their feet. She looked off into the distance and he watched her beauty shimmer as anger added another dimension to her loveliness, set the fire and ice to boiling.

"For someone who wanted to talk, you're awful damn quiet," he commented.

She dismounted, turned to him, and he slid from the saddle to face her. "You'd like to tell me I have some kind of obsession about the Arabians," she said. "But you can't."

"Why can't I?" he inquired.

The black eyes flared. "Because you understand. Down deep inside, you understand," she flung back. He kept his face impassive even as he silently swore at her acuity. "You know what it means. You know what we have preserved here. You have the feel for it inside you, Fargo. You understand, and yet you want to take them with you."

"I told you, Bill Alderson isn't like the others. He won't ruin the lines," he answered.

"And what if something happens to him? What if he has to sell out? What happens to the horses then? You can't guarantee that can't happen. Besides, even if he is a good man, he doesn't have the knowledge and experience with these Arabians that we have passed down here from generation to generation," she said, gathered herself for a moment. "No, I cannot risk that, and I won't."

"Your pa decided to go along with Bill Alderson."

"My father and I disagree on many things, and with all

the problems in Mexico he has become hungry for money," she said. "Dammit, Fargo, you understand the things I've said. Why don't you listen to yourself?"

"I hired out for a job. I don't have the right to listen to myself," he said.

"You haven't the right *not* to listen to yourself. No one has that right," Isabel countered, and he smiled. She could fence well with words. "I'll give you reasons you can't turn from. The French want those Arabians. Once they're not my father's any longer, they will come after them. Álvarez wants them in his hands. He knows how much money they will bring him. And if you somehow escape the French and Álvarez, the Apache will take them from you before you are north of San Antonio."

"And if I get by the Apache?" he asked, watching her sharply.

She shrugged, her face a beautiful mask. "It is unlikely," she allowed.

"I've done a lot of unlikely things, honey," he said softly.

The beautiful mask tore from her face as she exploded in anger. "You are twice a fool, Fargo. You will not listen to your heart and you will not listen to your head," she accused.

"You through convincing?" he asked.

"Quite through," she snapped, black eyes flashing. "You're disappointed, I'm sure," she added waspishly.

"Some," he conceded. "Thought you'd do better than that." He saw her begin to answer, hesitate, consider her words, and the moment shattered as six riders appeared at the edge of the little basin, gold-and-green uniforms flashing in the sun, plumed hats jutting upward. Fargo's glance went to Isabel as she looked up at the six French cavalrymen, and he growled his question: "You set me up for this?"

"No. Why would I?" She frowned.

"I can't take any horses back if I'm in a French cell," he rasped.

"I never thought of that. I wouldn't fight that way," she said, hurt in her tone.

He looked away from her as the six cavalrymen came down the sloping sides of the small basin at a full gallop. All had their carbines raised and trained on him as he started to reach for the big Colt, but he pulled his hand back. Six galloping horsemen with rifles trained were too many to take head-on, and he waited as the soldiers came to a halt, half-surrounding him and Isabel.

Three dismounted as the other three kept their rifles trained on him. "The gun, throw it down," one of the men ordered.

Fargo lifted the Colt from its holster with two fingers, tossed it on the ground, and the Frenchman scooped it up. The soldier wore a sergeant's stripe, Fargo saw as the man peered at him.

"You are the Yankee," the soldier said. "The one Major Andrade looks for."

"You're not part of his troop?" Fargo asked.

"We are replacements, on our way to join his camp. But we were told to watch for you," the soldier said. "And here we find you and your woman. We are in luck."

"I'm not his woman and you've no right to hold me for anything," Isabel said sharply, stepped toward him. The soldier's arm shot out as he backhanded her across the face, a sharp, stinging blow. She staggered back, her cheek reddened.

"*Chienne!*" the trooper hissed. "You will not talk to me that way."

Isabel glared across at Fargo. "That satisfy you?" she flung at him as her cheek grew redder. She turned back to the soldier again, her black eyes blazing fury. "You'll

77

answer for this, you imbecile," she hissed, shot her hand out, and cracked it across the sergeant's face in return.

With a roar of surprise as much as rage, the sergeant leapt at her, arms reaching for her. Isabel ducked away from his first lunge, spun, and her right foot slipped. She went down, the sergeant atop her, cursing in French.

Fargo saw him flip her onto her back, smash his hand across her face in a vicious slap, start to tear at the buttons of her blouse. Fargo's foot caught him in the back of the head and the man's plumed hat flew off as he pitched forward and Isabel rolled out from under him. Fargo whirled, ducked, but the blow of the carbine butt caught him enough of a blow to send him to the ground. He shook his head, pulled himself to one knee, saw Isabel nearby and the sergeant regaining his feet. The man's mouth was drawn back in a snarl of fury as he picked up his carbine.

"I would kill you both, but it will be better for me if I bring you to the major alive," he said with harsh breathing as he held himself under control. "Tie them together so they can walk," he ordered his men.

Fargo stayed quiet as the two soldiers pulled Isabel over to him and he saw her eyes flick to the bruise on the edge of his temple.

"I'm sorry," she said.

"You've more temper than brains," he growled, watched the two soldiers use lariats to tie her left leg to his right one from thigh to knee, placing the final knot just above the knee.

The sergeant had mounted his horse and glared down at them. "You'll walk behind. If you fall, you get up by yourselves. If you fall too often, you'll feel the whip," he said, turned his horse, and Fargo watched the soldiers bring the Ovaro and the Arabian up to the front of the column.

"Let's go," he said to Isabel. "We'll be hobbling more than walking."

She started forward, almost fell and he caught her elbow. "We'll never do it," she said. "I can feel the whip already."

"Swing your other leg out the same time I swing mine. Once we get the rhythmn we can do it," he told her. He swung his left leg out and she did the same with her right. "Now together," he said, and they brought their bound limbs forward. It was halting and hard, and he heard her gasp in pain as she pulled on unused muscles, but they managed to strike a rhythm that propelled them forward as though they were some strange, three-legged crane. The French were a good dozen yards ahead on their horses, but the men kept a constant glance back.

"I'll never make it, Fargo," Isabel said. "My right leg is ready to collapse now."

"We won't have to make it all the way," he whispered, and saw her frown at him.

"You're just saying that. There's no way we can get away," she protested.

"I never just say things, honey," he growled, and she shot another frown at him, unwilling to let his words stir hope, he saw. The soldiers moved to the right of a stand of prickly pear and proceeded along a narrow stretch of land that turned out to be the top of a sloping drop that went down into a deep arroyo thick with heavy brush and dwarf sumac at the bottom. His glance swept the arroyo as it stretched forward and back. There was no way the horses could get down into it without coming in from the ends, the dirt sides too loose and too steep.

"Hear me," he said tersely, and Isabel lifted her head to him and he saw the pain and exhaustion in her face. "We're going to fall down together, tell them we have to rest. Just go forward with me, use your arms as a cushion," he said. He pushed his body out, upset the precarious balance, and felt himself topple forward, taking Isabel with him. She hit the ground beside him, gasped out a rush of air, and he quickly pulled her up to a sitting position, their tied legs stretched out awkwardly. He saw the French had halted, watched the sergeant detach himself from the others and ride back to them. "Got to rest," Fargo pleaded.

The man sneered. "You'll have plenty of time to rest in a cell," he said. "If you're not on your feet by the time I get back to the others, I'll have you dragged the rest of the way."

Fargo stayed silent as the man wheeled his horse and cantered back to where the rest of the soldiers waited. He let Isabel fling a whispered oath after him as, using her body to shield himself from their eyes, he pulled the double-edged throwing knife from the thin leather strap around his calf. He tucked the slender blade into his waist and got his one leg under him, pressed, felt his muscles protest, but managed to pull himself and Isabel upright. "Walk," he said, and she began again with him, falling into the stiff rhythm they had managed to master.

With one eye on the horsemen a dozen yards ahead, he slid the thin sharp blade from his waist and wedged it into the ropes that bound his leg to Isabel's. He saw her eyes widen as she watched him work the blade back and forth against the ropes, short, quick strokes. He felt the sharp edges of the blade quickly shred the ropes, and the top band gave way, loosened, but clung in place. He paused, the blade unseen between his leg and Isabel's, as one of the Frenchmen glanced back for an instant. Split seconds after the trooper glanced away again, Fargo cut deep with the knife and severed the second band of ropes. He had to pause again when another of the soldiers glanced back, waited, and then stabbed at the last knot with the tip of the blade until it came apart. He felt the loosened ropes coming apart, sliding downward, and one of the soldiers glanced back, frowned, reined up to shout the alarm.

"Let yourself roll," Fargo said to Isabel. "Don't try to stop yourself." He spun as the last of the leg ropes fell away, pushed Isabel with both hands. She went sideways, toppled over the edge of the ridge, and he went after her, his feet instantly going out from under him. He felt himself rolling, brushed past Isabel as his weight gave him added momentum. He closed his eyes, kept his arms to his sides as he rolled down the steep side, the loose soil pelting his face. A branch struck against him, then another, and he felt the slope grow shallower, his whirling slow as he reached the bottom. Brush hit against him, more branches and twigs caught at him, slowed him further until he came to a hard, jolting stop against the side of a tree. He opened his eyes in time to see Isabel roll past him, her leg hitting against him, and he heard her sharp cry of pain as she landed hard in a cluster of thick underbrush.

He pulled himself around, crawled to where she tried to sit up. "You all right?" he asked.

"I think so." She nodded. "Nothing broken, at least," she said. She bore a scrape along one arm and her blouse was ripped at the sides, letting him enjoy a glimpse of the side of one deliciously curving breast. She pulled herself up straighter and the rip closed.

Fargo heard the shouts from atop the ridge and the pounding of the hooves. "They'll go to the end, make their way down, and come in after us," he said. "Let's find cover." He rose, pulled Isabel to her feet, saw the blouse was torn down from one shoulder also, her cream-white olive-tinged skin starting to swell into the top of her breast. He tucked the thin throwing knife more securely into his belt and clambered down into the dwarf sumacs and the thick brush that covered the floor of the arroyo.

"There are still six of them, and now we haven't even a gun," Isabel said.

"I'll get a gun, and they're not going to be coming at me head on with their carbines aimed," Fargo told her, led her deeper into the brush. He pointed to a dense thicket. "In there," he said. "Keep hidden. If they do stumble onto you, don't try to run. Let them take you."

"Where will you be?" she said.

"Evening up the odds," he said, and pushed her into the thicket. He stepped back, peered at the brush, and satisfied she was as well hidden as possible, he made his way to the side of the arroyo and dropped to one knee behind the elongated leaves of a sumac.

He hadn't long to wait before he saw the French appear from the other end. They had spread out in a single line to stretch from one side of the arroyo to the other. Stupid, Fargo grunted silently. The sergeant was using standard search procedure without enough men to do so. The result was that each of the soldiers was isolated, without nearby support. But they were making his task easier for him, Fargo smiled. He rose to a crouch, the razor-sharp throwing blade in his hand. One of the *chasseurs* neared, his carbine held in both hands, ready to fire as he peered into the deep brush and the stands of the dwarf sumac.

Fargo picked a spot between two of the brass buttons on the fancy gold-and-green uniform, drew his arm back, waited a moment longer. The soldier came toward him, peering into the foliage, and Fargo saw the man start to frown, peer harder. He snapped his arm down, and the narrow blade, perfectly balanced, hurtled through the air. Fargo saw the soldier's eyes widen and he tried to turn away too late as the blade speared into his chest, stopped only by the hilt. Fargo leapt forward as the man toppled from his horse, seized the carbine before it hit the ground. He whirled, saw the nearest soldier glance toward him. He fired and the soldier seemed to blow from his horse as though a giant funnel of wind had caught him. But the shot had sent the others whirling their mounts around. Fargo took the third one and fired as the soldier brought his carbine around. The rifle dropped from his hands, hit the saddle horn, and bounced to the ground as the man fell forward in the saddle and slowly slid from the side of the horse. But Fargo didn't wait to see him hit the ground as he leapt on the horse, pressed himself low over the animal, and sent it racing back toward the end of the arroyo. A half-dozen shots were way off the mark and he continued to streak for the end of the arroyo, reached it to see the thick underbrush almost vanish and a path curve upwards back to the top of the ridge. He took the horse partway up the path, halted, and slid from the saddle. He had the carbine reloaded and ready as the first of the remaining three Frenchmen came out of the arroyo.

He fired and one halted, the plume on his cap trembling violently before he fell from his mount. The other two wheeled away, raced back into the arroyo, and Fargo glimpsed the sergeant outdistancing the other man. As he watched, certain both were racing to flee from the other end of the arroyo, he saw the sergeant veer off, followed the man, and heard his own bitter curse. Isabel had come out of the brush and the Frenchman had spotted her. She turned as Fargo watched, tried to run, but it was too late, the horse closing ground in seconds.

"Goddamn," Fargo swore as he leapt onto the horse and raced down the curved path, back into the arroyo.

The other soldier had come to a halt with the sergeant and Fargo saw they had Isabel between them, the sergeant holding her by her black hair against the side of his mount, his carbine held down and pressed against her collarbone. Fargo neared, slowed the horse to a walk.

He let plans take shape in his mind as he moved closer. He'd have to time every move with split-second precision, but first he had to trigger their reactions, make them dance to his tune even though they had Isabel hostage. He heard the sergeant call out, rasp commands. "Dismount and drop the gun or she is dead," the man said. "I'm still taking you back alive."

"Like hell," Fargo said, started to swing the carbine up to his shoulder.

The soldier reacted instantly, self-protection before discipline, fired a shot from his carbine. But he'd hurried the shot and was no marksman in the first place.

Fargo felt the bullet pass to his left, just as he'd expected, but he pitched forward in the saddle, let a gasp of pain escape his lips before he toppled from the horse. He hit the ground with the carbine cradled beside him, lay still, his eyes closed. But he peered out through tiny slits and saw the sergeant fling Isabel to the ground and start toward him. It was what he waited for, and he pulled the carbine up, saw the man start to rein up, surprise flooding his face.

"Bastard," Fargo growled as he fired. The sergeant took the almost-point-blank blast full in the chest. The gold-and-green uniform flew apart with the cascading pieces of breastbone and blood. Fargo didn't wait to watch him fall from his horse, swung the gun toward the last soldier, and saw the man fling his carbine away.

"No, no . . . s'il plaît á Dieu," the man screamed as he ran, his plumed hat falling to the ground.

Fargo lowered the carbine, let the trooper flee in

terror, watched the figure continue to race for the end of the arroyo. He let the carbine slide from his hands and rose, walked to where Isabel had just pushed herself to her feet.

Her black eyes were wide and he saw the trembling that shook her from head to toe. He reached out, gathered her to him, one big hand pressed against her back. She leaned against him, her breasts warm and soft, and he smelled the faintly musky odor of powder and fear combined, strangely provocative. He felt her stiffen, fight the trembling.

"I'm quite all right," she said, but it took an effort.

"Sure you are," he agreed. "You always shake this way, I noticed."

A sudden rush of breath came from her and he felt her body relax, press harder against him. "I'm sorry," she murmured. "I thought they'd gone and I came out. I almost did it for us."

"It worked out, that's all that counts," he told her. "I'm sorry about thinking you'd set me up."

Her trembling subsided and she pulled back, black eyes softer than he'd thought they could be. "You are a remarkable man, Fargo," she said. "Truly remarkable." He saw her eyes search his face. "Forget the Arabians, Fargo. Let us be friends," she said.

"Jesus, you've a one-track mind, honey," he said.

She shrugged. "It would be best that way," she said.

The tear in the blouse at the shoulder had pulled deeper and her left breast swelled beautifully upward, exposed almost down to the full point. "You're a beautiful woman. Let's be lovers," he said.

"You have the one-track mind," Isabel reproached.

He echoed her shrug, pressed his mouth over hers. She stayed unmoving, refusing to respond, and he pushed her lips open, felt her try to draw back. He let his

85

tongue dart forward and heard her quick gasp, felt her lips soften, and then she was pulling away, twisting from his grip. "No," she said. "I am not one of your peasant girls who make love as easy as they make tortillas."

"At least they're honest with themselves," he said.

"You have no right to say that," she said, hurt and anger flaring in the black eyes.

He laughed. "I don't need the right. I just need the knowing," he said.

She turned away, a half-pout on her lips. "Let us get out of here. It has the smell of death in it," she said.

He nodded agreement, started to walk toward the still form at the other side of the arroyo to retrieve his throwing knife. He paused beside the sergeant and took the Colt out of the man's waist.

"Rotten little bastard, wasn't he?" Fargo commented.

"The troops the French have sent here are their worst, I have been told. They keep their best at home," Isabel said, and waited as he retrieved the knife.

They found the Ovaro and the Arabian tethered to a branch halfway up the curved path at the end of the arroyo. Fargo swung onto the horse, let his eyes sweep the ridge and the land beyond. Nothing moved. He hadn't expected anything. The soldier was still racing to reach Major Andrade's camp, still thankful for being alive.

Isabel rode in silence beside him as he headed north back to the ranch. The day was drifting to an end as they rode past the iron gate and he glimpsed María hanging wash beside the little clay hut, saw Isabel flick a glance at the girl. "You're not asking me to spend the night?" he remarked as he halted before the main house.

Isabel's eyes met the amusement in his glance with a contained mask over the black orbs. "Of course you may spend the night," she said evenly, refused to react to his chuckle.

"Some other time," he said. "Don't want to embarrass your pa if the major comes looking for me. And I want you to have a good night's sleep."

Her eyes narrowed at him, but she made no reply. He tossed her a grin, turned the Ovaro, and started to leave. "Fargo . . ." he heard her call, paused, looked back. The black eyes were round and soft, the contained mask gone from the delicately modeled face. "Thank you," she said softly.

He nodded and turned, sent the Ovaro into a trot, and rode out through the open gates, not glancing back. He headed the horse toward the Rio Grande, crossed the river as night fell, and rode into Laredo soon after. Hardly a vacation spot, it nonetheless offered a hot meal, a real bed, and waking without the chance of a French bayonet in his face. He left the Ovaro at the town stable to be washed and rubbed down, and found a hotel room for himself. He slept quickly, dreamed of soft eyes and soft arms, woke to realize he didn't know to whom they had belonged. Yesterday or tomorrow, he wondered as he washed and dressed, memories or anticipation. Maybe it didn't make any difference, he reflected. Either one could keep a man warm.

He breakfasted and got the Ovaro from the stable, the horse gleaming with whiteness, glistening with its black fore and hind quarters. He rode through Laredo, more than one pair of eyes admiring the Ovaro, made his way to Sam Alderson's spread.

"They're on the way," the man told him. "Old George Eckhardt saw Hank and Tim up in Austin. Another day or two, I'd guess."

"Too long and not long enough," Fargo said.

"Whatever the hell that means," Alderson frowned.

"The difference between bayonets, bandits, and beavers, that's what it means," Fargo said as he rode away. He headed back to the Rio Grande, found the river less silt-filled and running more swiftly, and he picked a spot to ford, emerged a dozen yards downriver. On the way to the ranch he glimpsed two columns of dust in the distance, tall enough and thick enough to mean French patrols. When he reached the ranch, he saw Isabel in the corral with the Arabians, moving among the horses, stroking each, pausing to check ankles, hooves. She saw him and came to the fence, beautifully tall in a white tailored shirt and gray riding jodhpurs. Her eyes peered at him, searched, and he saw the question there.

"Soon," he said, and her lips pressed tight against each other. He saw not anger so much as dismay in her eyes.

"We must talk more," she said.

"Whenever," he agreed, heard the door of the main house open, and saw Don Miguel come out, a black shirt and black trousers adding to the striking handsomeness of his thin, austere countenance and white-gray hair.

"Isabel told me of the French soldiers. I am indebted to you, Señor Fargo," the man said. "They were new men who did not recognize my daughter, unfortunately. But Major Andrade seems to have made you a marked man."

"Maybe he'll back off. He's not doing well," Fargo said dryly.

"Perhaps, but unlikely. I suggest you try to get your *vaqueros* together and take the Arabians out of here," Don Miguel said.

"Soon," Fargo answered.

"Good," the man said, nodded. "Alfredo left on business yesterday, but I'm sure he joins me in thanking you for Isabel's safety." He began to turn away but halted as

María appeared and hurried toward them. Fargo saw the apprehension in her wide face.

"*Dispénseme,* Don Miguel," she said quickly. "I have a message for Señor Fargo. Álvarez wants to see him."

Fargo saw instant displeasure curl in Don Miguel's face. "Álvarez is sending messages here?" the man snapped.

María swallowed hard. "Last night, my cousin Sánchez came, just long enough to tell me Álvarez wants to see the *señor,*" she said.

"I am very displeased, María, very," Don Miguel said. "Álvarez's *villanos* here at the ranch. *Terrible!*"

"I am sorry, Don Miguel," María said contritely. "Suddenly he was at my door."

"What did he say, María?" Fargo cut in, and saw gratefulness in her eyes for the interruption.

"Go to the foot of the mountains. Someone will wait there to take you to Álvarez," she said.

"All right." Fargo nodded and María hurried away with a last quick glance at him.

"You are not going?" Don Miguel frowned as his eyes speared the big man beside him.

"Why not? I've time to kill," Fargo answered.

"You keep on involving yourself in our problems, Fargo. It will do you no good, I am afraid," Don Miguel said.

"I'm curious." Fargo shrugged.

"I fear the government forces and Major Andrade would interpret that curiosity as sympathy," the man said severely.

"How do you interpret it, Don Miguel?" Fargo asked. "You've told me you are sympathetic to Juárez."

"Of course," Don Miguel said, and allowed a small smile that was more thin than warm. "Anything you could do to help the movement would be welcome, such

89

as saving that boy the other day. But I distrust men such as Álvarez. I think you should take care."

"I'll remember that." Fargo smiled affably.

Don Miguel nodded and walked on to the row of barns attached to the stable.

Fargo felt Isabel's eyes on him. "Got anything more to add?" he asked her.

"Be careful," she said, her lovely face grave.

"You sound as if you mean that," he said.

"I do," Isabel answered.

"Changed your mind about my taking the Arabs?" he grinned.

Her lovely face remained grave. "No," she said, "I won't change my mind on that. But these are dangerous men. I do not want to see you get yourself killed."

"I don't plan on doing that," he told her. She stepped back from the fence and he swung the Ovaro around. He saw her walking among the Arabians, determinedly not watching as he rode away. The fire might just break through the ice yet, he thought as he set the Ovaro into a fast canter.

The morning was gone when he reached the base of the rock mountains. He could have gone on, found Álvarez's camp on his own, but he halted, a sudden, strange premonition stabbing at him, telling him it was best that Álvarez not realize that. He sat his horse quietly, waited, and suddenly a horseman came into view on a ledge of rock above him, a thin figure weighed down with cartridge belts and an oversize *sombrero*. The man beckoned and Fargo fell in behind him. He stayed a half-dozen paces back and seemed to be simply following, though his eyes, as always, took in every natural marker, every turn and twist in the rock passages.

When they reached the flat table of stone, the man led the way through a passageway at the far end between two rock walls. Fargo took note of two other passages cut through the rock that seemed to lead to the same place, and he moved closer to his guide as the passage emerged onto a small plateau where a tent had been erected to one side, the poles wedged into crevices in the rock. A half-dozen men sat around a black iron kettle that smelled of beef stew, and the others were scattered on blankets around the edges of the plateau. The short-legged ponies tethered together against the far wall of rock.

Fargo's glance moved upward to the stone mountains that rose above the camp, traveled along the walls, noted the passages that cut into the rocks. He brought his gaze back to the tent as the flap opened and Álvarez came out and walked toward him. Fargo slid from his horse to return the rebel leader's nod. The man's harsh intensity, the glittering coal-black eyes, and unsmiling, thin lips beneath the drooping mustache made even the simplest words take on grimness.

"You will be glad you came, Fargo," he said.

"I hope so," Fargo allowed.

"Your language is money, not politics, cash not causes," Álvarez said.

"Most times," Fargo agreed.

"Then we understand each other. We need your help and we will pay well for it," Álvarez said. "A shipment of gold is due. We must have it. Juárez sent a courier with the details for us. I went to meet him. He had been murdered not more than minutes before I got there. Once again, there was a leak."

"So there'll be a gold shipment coming, but you don't know how it's being brought in," Fargo said.

"Exactly," Álvarez said bitterly.

"But neither do the others. You said whoever killed

Juárez's courier had no time to get anything from him either." Fargo frowned. "You're all in the same boat."

"No, they have all the advantages. They have many soldiers, the French patrols that will watch everything, stop everything, search everything. I cannot do that. If I tried, they would have me in no time. My men and I can only hide here, come out to raid, to hit and run back into these mountains. For the present, at least. Someday it will be different, but that time is not yet. That is why I have called for you," Álvarez said. "I need someone to find the gold shipment and then we will come down to get it."

"Why me?" Fargo asked.

"Because I have been told you are called the Trailsman in your country, that you see what other men do not see, that you are the very best," Álvarez said. "Find the shipment for us and I will give you ten percent of the gold. The shipment has to be a large one. Ten percent will be a lot of gold, *señor*."

Fargo felt his lips purse. "I'd imagine so," he agreed.

"For you, it will be another job for good pay, nothing more, nothing less. You will not be taking sides," Álvarez said.

Fargo smiled inwardly; the words were true enough, though he was sure the French wouldn't see it that way. "The shipment is due when?" he asked.

"Today, tomorrow, perhaps it is waiting now. Time is vital," Álvarez said.

Fargo let his thoughts turn for a moment longer. There was never anything wrong in picking up an extra buck, and this would mean a lot of extra bucks. It would also make all his waiting around worthwhile. "I find the shipment for you. You come and get it," he said.

"That is right." Álvarez nodded.

"You're on," Fargo said. "Any idea who murdered the courier?"

"Alfredo Cosaldo-López," the man bit out.

"Your guess?" Fargo pressed.

"He was seen near the spot only an hour before," Álvarez said.

"That makes it a guess," Fargo snapped.

"Good enough for me," the rebel leader said.

"Not for me," Fargo disagreed, and swung onto the Ovaro. "I'll get word to you when I can," he said.

Álvarez nodded. "Find the shipment. We will do the rest," he said, and motioned to the man with the oversize *sombrero*. "Take the *señor* back down," he ordered. The man moved his pony forward at once and Fargo followed through the narrow passage in the rock walls, stayed behind him as they retraced steps.

They were nearing the bottom of the rock mountains when Fargo spoke. "I'll find the rest of the way from here," he said.

The Mexican nodded, turned his pony, and disappeared up into the rocks.

Fargo let his thoughts revolve as he rode out of the mountains and across the dry, hot ground toward the ranch. There'd be no need to look for a lone rider carrying a pouch. That much gold had to come by wagon, maybe more than one. But the French would know that, too, he grunted. He would have to hang back, watch, let the French run down wagons. It was a calculated risk. If they found the shipment, Álvarez hadn't enough men to take it back. Yet he'd little choice. He'd count on their looking but not seeing.

Alfredo came from the house as he rode into the ranch, Don Miguel following. The younger man's weak but crafty face showed displeasure and he flung words out at once. "You are friends with Álvarez now?" he said.

"Wouldn't say that," Fargo replied calmly, and saw Isabel step from the house and stay by the door, watching, listening.

"What would you say?" Alfredo pushed at him with a half-sneer in his voice.

"He hired me to do a job for him. Good money. I never turn down good money," Fargo said.

"A job for Álvarez? No, *señor*, no. You've no right to take money from Álvarez," Alfredo said hotly.

"You giving me orders?" Fargo said softly. The younger man was too caught up in his own anger to notice the thin layer of frost that had slipped over the big man's lake-blue eyes.

Don Miguel was more observant.

"Of course not, Señor Fargo," he intervened quickly. "Alfredo did not mean that. You are free to do whatever you wish. You see your actions as simply a matter of a good paycheck. But Alfredo has deep feelings on this matter and so to him there are principles involved."

"I think principles is a word Señor Fargo does not include in his vocabulary," Alfredo bit out.

"I think careful is a word you'd better include in yours," Fargo said evenly.

Alfredo's lips quivered as he spun on his heels and stalked into the house.

Don Miguel's smile was apologetically pleasant. "Youth," he said. "Always so intense." He regarded Fargo with almost idle curiosity. "What is this task for which Álvarez has hired you? Or is that confidential?" He smiled.

Fargo had expected the question and decided on his answer. "Can't see it being a secret from you." He shrugged. "There's a gold shipment due, but the courier from Juárez with the details was murdered. Álvarez wants me to find the shipment."

Don Miguel shook his head sadly. "Once more things have gone wrong, it seems," he said. "And I fear the French will find that shipment first."

"Maybe not," Fargo said.

Don Miguel shrugged, smiled. "Good luck," he said as he strolled back to the house.

Fargo let his eyes go to Isabel as she continued to stay near the door, peering at him with questions in her black eyes.

"Go on, say it, whatever it is." He smiled, and she stepped closer to him.

"You say it's all just the money with you. I wonder if it is," she thought aloud.

He laughed. "You think I've become a Juarista?"

"No, I know better than that. Maybe you just like risking your neck," she said.

"Could be. And maybe I'm just curious about something," he said.

"What will finding out do for you?" Isabel asked.

"Make me feel better. I always like knowing I've figured something right."

"That's enough to make you risk your neck?"

"I'm risking my neck for the money," he said as he swung into the saddle.

"Where are you going now?" Isabel questioned.

"Start looking. There's plenty of light left," he said, and wheeled the Ovaro away. He saw Isabel spin on her heel and stride into the house, and he reined up outside the little clay house. María opened the door at once. He told her of the meeting with Álvarez in a few quick sentences. María's round brown eyes stared back at him.

"You do not do this just for the money," she said, but there was no question in her tone, no uncertain wondering. "Just the way you helped Felipe and me in Laredo. You did that because of something inside you."

95

He laughed. "Never liked one-sided fights," he said. "Or liars." He spurred the Ovaro on, rode quickly from the ranch, and headed toward the Rio Grande. He surveyed the terrain and found a low hill that was nonetheless high enough, with a lone twisted hackberry on it, to afford a long view up and down both sides of the river. He halted, settled down to wait, and saw three riders cross the river from the American side, traveling light, not even saddlebags with them. They turned east along the riverbank and he watched them ride out of sight. A thin spiral of dust preceded a column of French troops that appeared, rode along the riverbank. They plainly were on patrol as they rode west out of sight and were almost immediately followed by another squad that patrolled in the other direction.

He watched as the first squad returned, halted, and dismounted as the dusk began to send a lavender curtain over the land. They encamped, and the second squad reappeared, making camp a half-mile downriver. The troopers settled down in evenly spaced positions a half-dozen yards back from the riverbank.

Fargo pulled the Ovaro around and began to move away from the low hill. He had executed a wide circle away from the French squads when he saw a figure astride the white Arabian, looking ghostly in the twilight and headed toward it. Isabel stayed, let him reach her, sat very straight and tall in the saddle as he admired the regal beauty of her. "What are you doing out here?" he asked.

"Watching the watcher," she said.

"Why?"

"I was curious if you were really going to take up watch," she answered.

"Satisfied?" he asked. She nodded. "You can go home," he said. "I'm through for the night."

"That makes me more curious," she said.

"Why?"

"Aren't you afraid the shipment may slip through under cover of night?" she questioned.

He smiled. "No," he said, and gestured back to the French patrols dug in near the river. "That's what they're thinking, too. That's encouraging."

He saw her eyes narrow as she frowned. "Exactly what does that mean?" she slid at him.

"It means they don't think past their noses. You neither," he said, saw her eyes flare.

"Why wouldn't they try to move the gold in by night?" she snapped.

"Too risky. If they were spotted trying to sneak a wagon through by night, the game would be over. Their only chance is to be bold, move by day. They'll have some kind of cover. They've got to hope it'll stand up. But a wagon sneaking in at night would be a sure giveaway," he said.

Her black eyes peered at him. "To see what others don't see," she murmured. "To understand what others fail to understand."

"Just takes a little practice." He grinned.

"Don't be modest. That's out of character," she returned. "Will you come back to the ranch for the night?"

His laugh held a wry edge. "I think my welcome's kind of worn thin there," he said. " 'Less you're figuring to hide me in your room."

She ignored his remark. "Where will you go?"

"Up there," he said, nodding south through the last of the dusk. "Some good black persimmon trees there. Make a nice spot to bed down."

"And tomorrow? More watching?"

"Watching and finding, I hope," he said.

"Good night, Fargo," Isabel said, her beautifully modeled face staying composed, contained. She turned the Arabian and cantered away, headed back toward the ranch. He moved on when she vanished in the darkness, rode through the warm night till he found the cluster of black persimmons. They stood on a little hillock that gave him a clear view in every direction, and he laid out his bedroll, ate some beef jerky, washed it down with water from his canteen. The warm night wind blew softly and he undressed to his shorts, stretched out on the bedroll, the big Colt beside him. A Mexican wolf howled in the distance as he dozed under the winds that never cooled and slept the sleep of a puma, drawing in rest yet with the senses alert.

He snapped his eyes open as the sound came to him, faint at first, yet unmistakable: a horse, moving very slowly. It would have been unheard in many places, but here the dry, hard ground echoed each step. Fargo rose to one elbow, the Colt in his hand, his eyes sweeping the moonlit terrain below, and he located the horse, moving sideways to the trees, then turning, coming toward him. He watched it draw near and slid the Colt back into its holster on the bedroll.

He stayed stretched out on one elbow as the horse halted, the rider tossing onyx hair that fell across the shoulders of a white shirt.

"Couldn't sleep," she said as she slid from the horse. He saw her eyes move over the lean, clean muscled line of his body, pause for the briefest of moments at the bulge under his shorts. "I'll wait till you put trousers on," she offered.

"Don't plan to put on any," he said. "The air feels good on me."

Isabel's glance held a hint of disapproval, but her eyes lingered on his chest, the powerful rippled muscles of his shoulders, appreciation pushing aside reproach. She sank to her knees on the edge of the bedroll. "I want to talk to you," she said.

"I'm listening," he answered.

"I've a proposition for you," she began.

"Sounds good already," he said.

"Not that kind of proposition," she snapped.

"Doesn't sound as good suddenly," he said.

"You're being paid to bring the Arabians back. I'll pay you three times as much to leave them," she said.

He didn't answer, watching her black eyes examine him.

"You say you do things for money. All right, I'm making it more worthwhile to forget the horses than to take them," she said.

"I hire out, honey, but I don't go back on my word," Fargo said. "Money talks, but not that loud."

"Dammit, Fargo, I'm trying to find a way out of this," she said, sudden desperation in her voice.

He peered at her, turned the remark on his mind. It held a lot more unsaid in it.

"I mean, I'm trying another way to convince you," she said quickly. He kept his smile inside himself. She was trying to ride over words. He saw her lips soften, a wave of something close to despair sweep over her. "I thought you understood how I feel and why," she said.

"I understand. Doesn't change anything," he said.

"You take money from Álvarez, from your Bill Alderson, but you won't take it from me," she accused, and managed to look hurt. No act, he decided as he watched her.

"You want more than they do," he said. "They just want what I can do. You want what I am."

"Maybe María understands you better," she snapped.

"Maybe she tries more," Fargo said.

Her eyes flashed black fire as her arms came up and he felt the heat of her hands on his shoulders. Her mouth pressed his—soft, eager—and surprise held his response for an instant and then he kissed her back, his lips opening. She held a moment longer, then pushed away, stood up, and he watched the way her breasts rose and fell, pulled hard against the shirt as she drew in deep breaths. "Is that the kind of trying you understand?"

"It helps," he said mildly.

"Well, I won't convince you that way," she returned angrily.

He shrugged. "Can't think of a better way," he said.

She flung a glare back, spun and pulled herself onto the horse. "I will," she said, sent the Arabian into a gallop.

He watched her virtually fly across the night terrain, disappear into the darkness. He lay back and the taste of her lingered on his lips, her words in his thoughts. "I'm trying to find a way out of this," she had thrown at him. Not just the impasse between them, he was certain. Something more, something darker. He let his thoughts turn over, idly drift. Isabel was much like this Mexico of hers, full of turbulent smolderings, a powder keg. She had turned away from most of it, wrapped herself in her own obsession. And now that was about to explode from under her also. She wouldn't just let it happen. The fire and the ice would see to that. He turned on his side, one hand on the Colt, and sleep swept over his long, muscled form.

5

He watched the French patrols leave their camps along the river as the new day rose, the hackberry on the low hill providing just enough shade from the hot morning sun. The two squads mounted up and set off in opposite directions to patrol along the river. Other patrols would be patroling back farther inland, he was certain. The low hill gave him more than enough height to view the land and the river, and he settled down to wait, watched the new sun climb higher into the sky. He saw her coming out of the south, in the direction of the ranch, and he swore softly as she guided the horse up to where he waited beneath the hackberry. She rode a deep-brown bay and he was grateful for that much.

His eyes were hard as she halted beside him. "Get away from here," he growled.

Isabel's thin brows arched disdainfully. "This is my country. I go where I please," she said.

"Who sent you here?" he pressed.

"Nobody." she frowned, flared in anger. "You think Alfredo put me up to this, don't you?"

"I didn't say that," he answered. "But somebody doesn't want Álvarez to get that gold."

"Nobody sent me. I came on my own," she said.

"Why?"

"I can't believe you can spot a gold shipment the

French patrols won't spot first, not right under their noses. I want to see for myself," she said.

"You won't see and you won't know," he told her, letting his eyes travel up and down her tall, lovely form. She'd had the sense to put on a dark-green shirt and matching riding skirt, he grunted silently. "You get in my way, I'll stuff you in this tree," he warned, turned from her, and let his eyes sweep the riverbank. Two wagons appeared on the Texas side of the river, heavy drays with high, chain-linked stake sides, each filled high with wooden kegs, two big draft horses pulling each. He watched as they pulled up at the narrowest and shallowest part of the river, slowly and carefully eased their way across. The shallowest section was nonetheless deep enough to entirely cover the wagon wheels, he noted. They moved slowly across the sluggish waters, pulled up on the Mexican side, let the horses rest a moment, and started inland. Fargo followed with his eyes, saw the two big drays swing south when the French patrol descended on them.

He watched as the patrol halted the wagons, dismounted, began to unload each and every keg. He could hear the drivers shouting protests. "Goddammit, they're on the way to Durango. They got water problems there," he heard one of the driver's shout. But the French opened each keg, peered inside until they were finished, tossed the kegs back onto the wagons with considerably less neatness than they had been packed. The two big drays rolled away and Fargo felt Isabel's eyes on him as she tried to read behind the chiseled impassiveness of his face. She'd not get far, he knew, and felt her irritation as she realized as much and turned away.

He watched two riders move along the Mexican side of the Rio Grande and go their way. A battered light Concord coach came along the Mexican side of the river, a driver and brakeman atop, three passengers visible through the paneless windows and a half-dozen bags and a strongbox on the roof. A small French patrol caught up to it, waved it down. They made the three passengers get out, searched the trio, made the driver open the strongbox and the other bags. Satisfied, they sent the coach on its way north along the riverbank.

Two boys driving a flatbed farm wagon piled high with square bales of hay rumbled slowly west some hundred yards back of the riverbank. The French patrol appeared, halted it, and Fargo watched the soldiers use their bayonets to stab into each bale a half-dozen times, finally let the wagon go on. "Two boys with hay," Isabel sniffed. "How ridiculous to waste time on that."

"Nothing ridiculous about it," Fargo said. "If I were trying to sneak over a gold shipment, I'd use the least likely disguise I could find."

He saw her delicate brows come together in a furrow as she speared him with a sharp glance. "You think that hay wagon could be the shipment?" she asked.

"Didn't say that," he answered, turned from her as another wagon appeared on the Texas side of the border. Fargo's eyes took in the fresh red-paint job with the gilt trim, the upraised rear panel, and the double sliding doors in front. A single gray horse pulled the wagon toward the river, the driver wearing a tattered frock coat and a beaver Wellington on his head. As the wagon turned to parallel the riverbank, he read the gold letters on its side:

REMEDIES AND MEDICINES
For Young and Old

"Converted butcher wagon," he said. "Patent medicine man's rig now."

"Or something else," Isabel remarked.

He shrugged, watched the driver find the shallow spot in the river and take the wagon across into Mexican territory. The wagon moved straight south and he saw a squad of French *chasseurs* spot it, move toward it, halt it a few hundred yards from the river. The soldiers opened the rear panel fully, pushed back the sliding front doors. Some went inside and brought out boxes, trunks, opened everything. They pressed the side panels of the converted wagon, took up the driver's seat to peer beneath it. They rode off and left the medicine salesman to put everything back in place.

Traffic slowed and the noon sun kept most travelers in the shade. Isabel fished some good cold beef from a sack on her saddle, offered him some, which he ate in silence beside her.

"Your eyes haven't stopped moving back and forth, along the river, out to the horizon," she commented.

"That's right," he said.

"It still makes no sense. You're just sitting here and watching. If they find the gold shipment, you'll see them do it. But you won't have it. They will," she said.

"Maybe," he said.

"Maybe what?" she snapped testily.

"Maybe they won't keep it and maybe they won't find it," he said.

"It hasn't been any of the wagons they've checked so far," she said.

"Maybe no and maybe yes," he said, saw her peer hard at him at once and lapse into silence. He leaned back on the hilltop, stretched, sat up, rose to one knee suddenly.

Isabel followed his gaze and saw two old Conestogas slowly moving from upriver on the Mexican side. They drew closer, two horses pulling each, a woman and a man in the first one, two young boys in the second, one hold-

104

ing the reins. Fargo's eyes narrowed as he saw the undersides of the wagons streaked with dark places.

"What is it?" Isabel said, picking up his alertness instantly.

"They crossed up a ways, far enough up for the wagons to just about dry out," he said. He watched as the two old, splintered Conestogas slowly turned away from the riverbank and started south. The rock mountain fastness lay directly south, he mused. The two wagons had gone almost a quarter of a mile when the patrol appeared, brought them to a halt.

Fargo watched, standing on his feet, as the French had the man and the woman drag everything they had out of the two Conestogas. Household pieces; two wooden chests, which they had to open; and a small pump organ carried in the second wagon. The French examined each piece of wearing apparel, each hatbox, and tested the two large water casks on each wagon. When they left, it took the man, the woman, and the two boys over an hour to put everything back in the Conestogas. They continued south slowly, one following the other.

Again, Fargo saw Isabel peering at him, trying to read his thoughts, and again she turned away with a sniff of irritation. The afternoon had reached the midpoint when one of the French patrols rode into sight and halted not far away at the edge of the river. The men dismounted, let their mounts stand in the water to cool their ankles. Fargo heard sounds, unmistakable, from the other side of the river, and his eyes went to the ridged steps of the Texas countryside where yucca, cholla, dry thick brush, and cedar elm afforded fair cover. The half-screams, half-shouts resounded in the air, the very individual cries of Indians riding hard on the chase. Then he saw the wagon, a big, long high-sided dead-axle dray, a six-mule team pulling hard, one man on the reins, another beside him with a rifle, a third at the back of the wagon, rifle in hand. A canvas had ripped partly away to reveal the wagon carried a full load of borax. On a ridge above the borax team, he saw three Indians appear, long, greased black hair, dark rather than bronzed skins, then another three coming in from below the wagon to cut it off.

He saw the French troops on their feet, watching, rifles raised but holding their fire. The driver of the wagon swerved his six-mule team away from the ridge as three arrows struck hard into the side of the heavy dray. He headed the team directly for the river as the pursuing Indians shifted to follow, those on the ridge slow in joining in the chase.

"Apache?" Fargo heard Isabel gasp.

His eyes speared the pursuing Indians, who rode wildly rather than effectively. "No, Tonkawa, I'd guess. Small potatoes compared to the Apache," he said. "But an arrow's an arrow," he added.

The driver whipped his six-mule team down the slope, headed straight toward the river as the Tonkawa swung in behind him. Fargo saw the French soldiers beckoning to him to cross to their protection. The driver neared the river, suddenly yanked leather, and the mules swung to the right just short of the water as he turned the wagon to roll along the edge of the riverbank. The pursuing Tonkawa shifted directions, swung after the wagon, and Fargo saw the three men on the wagon duck low to avoid a volley of shots. The French soldiers continued to beckon and shout, but the driver wheeled the mules again, a wide circle to the right, came around to send the wagon racing back in the other direction along the bank. He swerved toward the river as the Indians raced at him, swerved again as the mules got their feet wet and continued to race along the bank.

Fargo swung onto the Ovaro. "You keep your ass right

here," he flung at Isabel, and sent the horse into a full gallop as he raced down the low hillside. The Tonkawa were closing in on the wagon as he hit the water, and he was in midriver when he fired a volley of shots from the Colt, saw the Indians rein up, turn in surprise. He reached the Texas bank, reloading as he did so, fired again, and one of the Tonkawa flew from his pony, long, heavily greased hair bouncing in the air.

The French troops began to fire from their side, volleys that made up in quantity what they lacked in accuracy. Fargo raced the Ovaro toward the Indians, winged another one, who managed to maintain his seat on the horse as he clutched his arm. He saw the others wheel in a tight circle, suddenly uncertain if the French were going to cross or if the big man charging at them had friends coming. They turned, broke off further pursuit, and charged up the slope beyond the bank, swung onto the first ridge and vanished behind the brush.

The borax wagon rolled to a halt and Fargo halted beside it. The canvas had been all but completely ripped away now and small pieces of the white, powdery-surfaced borax spilled from the high sides of the wagon.

"Much obliged, mister," the driver said as he let the reins drop and breathed a long sigh.

"Goes for me, too," the other man said, pushed his hat back. They were both Americans, Fargo noted, while the man in the rear lying atop the borax was an olive-skinned Mexican, sporting a flat-brimmed *poblano*. "They got Chico, my other loader," the driver said. "Come down on us out of those ridges back a piece. Can't see what they'd want with a load of borax."

"Wasn't the borax," Fargo said. "They wanted four guns, whatever else they could take from your carcasses, and maybe the mules." He let his glance move across the pyramid of borax that filled the wagon. "You were heading right for the river. Why didn't you go across? They wouldn't have gone after you with the French waiting there," he asked.

"Couldn't risk the wagon. We can't cross till low tide. This is one heavy load. We could've gone into a mud hole and lost the whole load. I've got to cross at low tide, when I can see some," the driver explained.

"You do figure to cross, then," Fargo said.

"Yep, we're headed for Neuva León, but when it's low tide," the man said.

Fargo's glance moved to the side as one of the French soldiers rode into midriver, halted, his eyes moving from the driver to Fargo and back to the driver.

"You were lucky, m'sieu," he said, and Fargo noted the corporal's stripes on his sleeve. "You should have come across. We would have protected you."

"Told this gent, we couldn't risk the wagon. We'll wait for low tide," the driver said.

The soldier's glance went to Fargo and the Ovaro. "You are the one Major Andrade wants. He described your horse," the corporal said.

"Where is the major?" Fargo asked. "Haven't seen him with any of the patrols."

"In camp. A supply wagon rolled and struck him, injured his leg. He will be all right in a few days," the man said.

"Too bad," Fargo commented.

"You are lucky, m'sieu," the soldier said. "We have more important things to do than bother with you now." He turned and made his way back to the Mexican side of the river.

Fargo glanced at the wagon driver. "We'll just stay here, thank God for being alive, and wait for low tide," the man said. "That'll be about four o'clock, I'd guess."

"Just about," Fargo agreed. "Take care, now."

"Much obliged again, mister," the man said as Fargo

turned the Ovaro and started up the riverbank, rode far enough to find a spot to cross not directly in front of the French patrol. He emerged onto Mexican soil, made a wide circle, returned to the low hill from the back side, and saw Isabel get to her feet, her eyes follow him as he reached her.

"Now what?" she asked.

"We keep watching and waiting," he said, slid to the ground, and stretched out to lean against the hackberry.

"There's been nothing. Maybe you're at the wrong spot," she said.

"Right spot," he grunted.

"Dammit, you can't be sure of that," Isabel flared.

"Álvarez is in the mountains straight south. This is the nearest spot to cross to meet him, not miles up or down," Fargo said.

She lapsed into silence, sat beside him until he leaned forward as a two-wheeled, closed sedan cab came into sight, pulled smartly by a light-boned brown carriage horse, moving along the Mexican side of the border. A woman drove, and the French patrol, which had been idling by the bank, came to attention, halted the sedan cab with politeness. They opened the closed doors, searched the inside of the cab, looked into the roof panel, finally let her go on with bows.

Fargo glanced at the sun, saw it moving quickly down the long corridor, and his glance went to the river. It had grown sluggish, down at the banks at least a foot. He rose as the driver of the borax wagon snapped the reins over the team of mules. He guided the team to the edge of the bank, picked the shallowest spot, slowly eased the wagon into the water. The low tide didn't reach beyond the middle of the wagon wheels as the mules pulled their way through the water, finally emerging onto the opposite bank. Fargo watched as the French surrounded the wagon for a few moments, saw just what he had seen, a heavily loaded dead-axle dray piled high with the powdery-surfaced borax, solid flat sides, and plate-metal bottom, everything open to the eye. They waved the borax team on and Fargo watched the mules slowly head across the flatland as dusk began to creep in from the horizon.

He turned away, took the Ovaro's reins, and Isabel frowned at him. "So soon?" she asked.

"Be dark in fifteen minutes. You can go home now," he said.

A note of smugness came into her lovely features. "I was right. They didn't find the shipment, and neither did you just standing up here watching," she said.

"It's here," he said. "It came through." He saw her eyes widen.

"No, impossible," she said.

"It came through," he repeated.

Her eyes searched his face. "One of those wagons?" she questioned. His silence was its own answer. "It can't be. The French examined every one of them. I watched," Isabel protested.

"So they did," Fargo agreed as he climbed into the saddle.

Isabel pulled herself onto her horse at once, swung in beside him. "The first two wagons with the kegs of water," she said. "They looked in every keg."

"They never checked the bottoms, not one," Fargo said.

Her eyes widened excitedly. "That's where the gold is hidden?" she asked.

"Didn't say that," Fargo answered.

Her eyes narrowed at him. "No, you didn't," she said. "That light Concord coach, they searched everyone and every piece of luggage on it as well as inside it."

"They didn't check the water tank," he said.

"You think the gold was inside it?" she pressed.

"Didn't say that," he answered as the night blanketed the flatland, and he heard her little hiss of impatience.

"The two boys with the hay wagon, the French bayoneted every bale of hay," she said. "They found nothing."

"They bayoneted through the center of each bale," he pointed out.

"You saying the gold could have been at the bottom or the top of the bales?"

"Possible," he said.

She continued to try to read his face as she prodded further. "The Patent medicine man, they looked at everything he had in the wagon, checked the side panels and the rear drop," she said.

"Converted butcher wagon," Fargo grunted. "Butcher wagons usually have double floors for drainage."

She stared, taking in the import of his answer. "The two Conestogas, they checked the water tanks on both, searched every chest, hatbox, every piece of clothing. They looked everyplace," she said.

"Except inside that pump organ," Fargo said, and heard her gasp of breath as she stared wide-eyed at him.

"The borax wagon was all out in the open," she said.

"That's right," he agreed.

"And the Sedan cab with the woman, that was too small to hold a gold shipment hidden," Isabel said.

"I heard once about a thousand gold coins being hidden in hallowed-out shafts and hollowed wheel hubs," Fargo remarked.

She frowned at him. "Damn, Fargo, you've made any one of them possible," she said.

"Your guess," he said.

"But you know," she pressed.

"I know," he said grimly. He felt the frustration in her angry silence as the ranch came into sight, knew she was spinning thoughts inside her, trying to make a choice, find something to hang her decision on. She broke the silence as they reached the main house, an explosion of chagrin and frustration.

"I saw everything you saw, dammit," she hissed.

"Correction," he said, a faint smile touching his lips. "You looked. I saw," he said.

Her lovely lips bit down on each other as she tried to search his face.

The door of the house came open and Alfredo emerged, Don Miguel following. Alfredo's frown went to his sister first. "Where have you been all day? We were worried," he said.

"With him. Watching," she said.

The younger man turned, the sneer instant on his face. "So you found nothing for your new employer, Señor Álvarez," he said.

"Found what he wanted me to find," Fargo said calmly and saw Alfredo's jaw drop.

"You found the shipment?" he breathed.

Fargo saw Don Miguel's brow arch in surprise, almost amusement, and his eyes go to Isabel as if for confirmation.

"I saw nothing," she said almost sullenly.

"Álvarez is to meet me in a little more than an hour," Fargo said. "In the trees at the top of that arroyo south of here. I'll tell him then and he'll do the rest."

"You have earned your money, it seems," Alfredo said.

"It seems," Fargo agreed. "I'll be moving on, in case he's early."

"Álvarez will be glad. This will be the first shipment

112

that has gotten through to him in a long while," Don Miguel said.

"Guess so," Fargo said blandly, and watched as Alfredo spun on his heel and strode into the house, flinging anger behind him. Don Miguel's smile was apologetic as he followed his son inside. Isabel's black eyes stayed on the big man beside her.

"Which wagon was it? What did you see?" she asked.

"I will say nothing. You have my promise on that."

"When it's over," he said.

He saw as much hurt as anger come into the black orbs. "I don't break promises," she said.

"And you don't know who's listening right now," he said, saw her eyes flick to the blackness surrounding them, the deep shadows of fences and stables. "When it's over," he said as he wheeled the Ovaro and set off in a fast canter. He looked back, saw her dismount and go into the house.

He rode a half-circle, came back from the other side, dismounted as he neared the clay hut. He kept the Ovaro out of sight behind the little house and slipped around to the door to knock softly.

María answered, surprise in her eyes as he slipped inside.

"Listen to me," he said tersely. "Get a horse and go to Álvarez. Tell him exactly what I tell you, understand?" She nodded and he gave her instructions, details, and when he finished, she nodded, took a shawl to put around her shoulders. He opened the door a crack, saw the night was empty, and slipped outside. This time he rode straight, headed for the thicket of trees where the arroyo began. He rode at a gallop, the pinto's powerful stride shrinking the distance. The ridge came into sight, the arroyo a black pit below and then the thicket of trees.

Fargo rode into the center of the trees, jumped to the

113

ground, and took off his hat and jacket. He pulled a piece of branch down, enough stems on it to serve his purpose. He positioned the jacket over the branch, the hat atop it, pushed the clothes and the branch back into the thicket, and stepped away. He brought the Ovaro under the clothes, tethered the horse, and stepped back again. In the darkness of the thicket, the disguise worked more than well enough. Someone stealing up to the thicket would think that he was waiting astride the Ovaro. He backed to one side of the thicket, knelt down in the deep shadows to wait. It would not be a long wait, he knew.

He half-closed his eyes, let his ears read the night, and heard the soft scurrying sound of a desert cottontail, the hum of a beetle. In the distance, the hissing snarl of a bobcat came to him, but mostly there was silence. The footsteps came to him first and he opened his eyes in surprise. The visitor had dismounted plenty far away, crept up on foot.

Fargo pulled the big Colt from its holster as the shadowed shape appeared. He felt his muscles grow tense as the figure came closer, stepping carefully through the thicket. The figure halted, still deep in the shadows, but Fargo saw the arm lift, point forward. The shot sounded as though a cannon had gone off in the little thicket, and Fargo saw the jacket over the Ovaro move. He straightened, stepped forward.

"Drop the gun, Don Miguel," he said softly, and saw the figure stiffen. Fargo stepped out of the shadows and the man slowly turned, his thin autocratic face and gray-white hair showing dimly yet clear enough in the faint moonlight that filtered into the thicket. "The gun," Fargo said, and Don Miguel let the pistol drop from his hand, his smile almost sad.

"You expected it would be me," he said.

Fargo nodded and kicked the gun away. "Hadn't much doubt," he said.

"Why? I am curious," the man said. "Why not Alfredo? He was certainly the most logical."

"Too logical," Fargo said. "His hate for the Juárez movement was no secret. Juárez would never have trusted him as a channel for information on shipments. But you had Juárez's trust. You came on as a believer, sympathetic to his movement."

"But you saw fit to doubt that. Why?" Don Miguel asked.

Fargo let a harsh sound escape his lips. "María and her brother. You didn't bat an eye about sending them in place of Isabel and Alfredo, though you knew it could've meant they'd be killed. That took a man who didn't give a damn about the peasants. Nobody who really believed in Juárez could've done it."

Don Miguel's little smile held rue in it. "A most astute observation, Señor Fargo. I am impressed," he said. "And now you will hold me here for Álvarez?"

"Álvarez isn't meeting me here. I sent María to him with word on the gold shipment. I'd guess he's picking it up about now," Fargo said. "But your double game is over. Álvarez will get word of it to Juárez. That's what I really cared about. I never like double-dealers, even aristocratic ones. I'll take you back to the ranch."

The man's lips pursed as Fargo shook his jacket and hat from the branch and swung onto the Ovaro, holding the Colt on him. Don Miguel walked back to where he had left his horse, climbed into the saddle, and Fargo rode behind him back to the ranch.

Isabel glanced out a window as they rode up to the house, and she came outside at once, Alfredo following. She saw the Colt in Fargo's hand, frowned at him as she glanced at her father. "What is it? What's happened?" she asked.

"I demand to know what you're doing holding a gun on my father," Alfredo said.

Fargo spun the big Colt in his hand, dropped it into his holster, swung from the saddle, watched Don Miguel's slender shape dismount. "You want to break it to them or should I?" he asked.

"Señor Fargo has uncovered a few facts," Don Miguel said, his aristocratic face losing none of its hauteur. He spoke in Spanish, quick short bursts of words aimed mostly at Isabel. He told the truth of what had happened, Fargo knew. He had only to watch Isabel's face to see that as the shock swept into her eyes, growing deeper, pain joining shock. Alfredo showed no surprise and Fargo hadn't expected any. He'd no doubt been well aware of the truth. But Isabel stared at her father when he finished, her eyes holding mostly pain now.

"And now what, Fargo?" Don Miguel said with sudden crispness. "I suppose I should be grateful to you for not shooting me at the arroyo."

"No point in it. You tried to blow me away, but I don't give a hoot in hell about that. We've some unfinished business," Fargo said.

"The Arabians," Don Miguel said.

"That's right." Fargo nodded. "I'll be taking them in another day, then you and Juárez and the French and Álvarez can all get on with your feudin' and fightin'."

"Agreed," Don Miguel said.

"You will be picking up your money from Álvarez before you leave us, of course," Alfredo sneered.

"Man earns his pay, he deserves to get it," Fargo said.

The younger man turned away, his face filled with bitter anger; Don Miguel followed him into the house. Fargo turned to Isabel, whose eyes regarded him sor-

rowfully. "I didn't know, not any of it. I never sus-
pected," she said, words coming hard.

"Never figured you did," he said, and started to pull
himself into the saddle.

"Will you come back in the morning? Please?" she
asked. "I'll want to talk then. I'll need someone to talk to.
Now I just want to be alone, to think, to give myself time
to believe all that's happened."

"I'll stop by," he agreed, starting to turn the Ovaro
away.

"Fargo . . ." she called. "Did the gold shipment really
come through or was it all planned just to trap my
father?"

"It came through," he said. "Álvarez has it by now."

"Which wagon?" she asked.

"The borax wagon," he said softly, and saw her lips
part in astonishment.

"But the borax was all there in plain sight. There was
no place to hide the gold," she protested.

"It was part of the borax, at the bottom, painted and
dusted with borax powder so the pieces looked just like
the borax," he told her.

"How did you notice it when no one else did?" she
asked.

"I didn't. They did a good job," he said.

"Then how did you know?"

"A man being chased by Indians out to lift his scalp
wouldn't hold back at crossing a river to safety, not unless
he had some damn special reason. The low-tide story was
true enough, but not because they were afraid of a mud
hole. They had to be sure the water would be low so it
wouldn't reach the bottom of the wagon and wash away
the powder and paint they'd dusted the gold pieces
with."

She stared at him, her black eyes round. "To see

where others don't see," she murmured. She turned, started into the house. The pain and shock still clung to her face, but she walked with her head held high, her sinuous figure tall and straight.

Fargo moved the Ovaro into the dark night, rode back to the line of black persimmons, and laid out his bedroll. Weariness swept over him as he cradled the big Colt beside him and drank in sleep.

6

The feel of it hung in the air when he reached the ranch in the late morning and his wild-creature sensitivity picked it up at once. Small knots of *vaqueros* clustered together, no activity in the corrals. Fargo rode in slowly, approached the main house, and had just swung from the saddle when Alfredo burst out, his weak face contorted with anger. He had a six-gun strapped on, a Walker Colt with a mother-of-pearl grip.

"You are proud of what you have done?" he shouted.

"What the hell are you talking about?" Fargo frowned, saw Don Miguel step from the house, his long face drawn in.

"I'm going to kill you," Alfredo snarled. His hand went to the holster.

"No," Don Miguel shouted, but Alfredo was drawing, his lips pulled back in a snarl. He had the pearl-handled pistol out of the holster when Fargo drew and fired with speed almost too quick for the eye to follow. The revolver flew from Alfredo's hand as he screamed in pain, grabbed at his thumb. He staggered backward, as much fear as surprise in his face.

"Stupid little bastard," Fargo growled. "I could've put it into your gut."

Don Miguel bounded down the few steps to come between Alfredo and the big man. "No, please . . . he is upset, we are all upset," he said, and turned to his son. "Go into the house. Have your thumb bandaged," he ordered, and Fargo saw Alfredo was quick to obey. Don Miguel turned back to face his blue-quartz eyes.

"Álvarez . . . he has Isabel," the man bit out.

"What?" Fargo frowned.

"A few of his men sneaked in just before dawn. She was asleep. We all were. They took her and left a note from Álvarez," Don Miguel said. "I am to turn all my lands, my income, my bank accounts, everything I own, over to Benito Juárez, or he will kill Isabel. And after I have done this, I am to go to him and he will release Isabel."

"Your life for hers," Fargo said.

"Sí." The man nodded. "Alfredo feels he would not have known about me and he would not have the gold to let him feel powerful again if it were not for you."

"Matter of time," Fargo said. "He knew there was a leak someplace. He'd have figured it sooner or later."

"He said one thing more. If I attack to try and save her, he will kill her at once," Don Miguel said. "I have till tomorrow to do what he says. Alfredo says to get the French and attack. He says Álvarez will be too busy defending himself to bother about Isabel."

"Alfredo's a damn fool. But then you know that. Álvarez could hold off an attack force for days in those mountains. He'd have plenty of time for Isabel," Fargo answered.

The man's hands fluttered helplessly. "I fear you are too right," he said. "I must think, talk again with Alfredo."

"Why Alfredo?" Fargo queried.

"Recently, I put half of everything I own in Alfredo's name. He is my only son. I must have his permission to sign everything over to Juárez," Don Miguel said, turned away, and started into the house.

"Shit," Fargo muttered. Alfredo was a selfish little weakling. He'd cry and moan and wring his hands all over the place, but he wouldn't be above letting Isabel go down the drain. He'd justify it in some way or another, call her a sacrifice to help keep Mexico out of the hands of Juárez. He could be righteous about it without half-trying.

Damn, Fargo swore under his breath as he turned away. He hadn't expected this. He wasn't taking on blame for it. The hatreds ran too deep here for him to trigger. But he'd let himself take part, a limited, confined part that had now blown out of hand. But, above all, there was Isabel, perhaps more of a pawn than anyone involved.

He swore again, leaned on one of the corral fences as his thoughts raced. Álvarez had set a deadline. He'd stick by it. Alfredo could anguish and delay till the decision was past deciding. That'd be another way out for him. Damn, Fargo swore again. Isabel had one chance, and he was it. One man could get into Álvarez's stronghold. One man had a chance, a man who knew the way. His thoughts broke off as he spied María hurrying toward him with a basket of wash under one arm, her wide, pretty face grave. She halted before him, set the basket down.

"I did not know he would do this, Fargo. I would have warned you," she said. "When he heard how Don Miguel had been the betrayer, the leak, he became wild. But I did not dream he would do this."

"You seem to know a good deal about him. I want two answers. He owes me ten percent of the gold. That'll be a sizable amount. Would he exchange it for Isabel? The movement needs all the money they can get," he asked.

"No," she said without hesitation.

"If Don Miguel agrees to everything and gives himself for Isabel, would Álvarez keep his word and let her go?"

Fargo saw her pause, her deep eyes blink at him. "He would kill them both," she said. "I told you, he is filled with hate. Alfredo and Don Miguel, if they had the chance, they would kill him as they would step on a *cucaracha*. He will do the same . . . or worse."

Fargo nodded slowly. He'd asked, and she'd given him his answer. He couldn't bring himself to say thanks. With that special brand of female intuition she picked up his thoughts at once. "You will go after her," María said.

He nodded. "Tonight. It's her only chance," he said.

"María's eyes held his. "You did not do this to her. Don Miguel did it. He played the jackal," she said.

"He wrote the book. I opened a page," Fargo said, touched her face with his hand.

"Álvarez, you will kill him if you have to?" she said.

"If I have to," he admitted.

She nodded in understanding and looked away, her eyes touched with a private pain.

"This bothers you, María," he said gently.

"He is my half-brother," she said, picked up the wash basket, and hurried away, not looking back.

"Shit," he murmured as he pulled himself onto the Ovaro. The people and the country were full of crosscurrents. He wanted out as fast as he could. After he tied up some loose ends.

He sent the pinto into a fast trot, headed north to the Rio Grande. The French had withdrawn their patrols, he saw. They'd probably learned that Álvarez had the gold. He crossed the river, swung onto Texas soil, and headed for Sam Alderson's spread. He was glad to see the line of horses tethered outside the main house; he hurried inside, where a roomful of wranglers greeted him.

"Been waiting for you." Sam Alderson laughed.

Fargo let a wry smile edge his lips. "I'm damn glad to see you all here," he said. "But I need another day, maybe two. Got myself into something I have to see through."

"Must be a woman involved," Alderson said.

"Give the man a cigar," Fargo said. "But not the way you're thinking. Her neck's on the line, not her beaver."

"With you, that could change." Alderson laughed.

Fargo shrugged. "If I get lucky," he said.

"Meanwhile, let me introduce you to the best damn bunch of wranglers west of the Mississippi," Alderson said. "You've met Tom Bessie. This here's Slim Staunton," he introduced. He went around the room, introduced each man.

None were young, Fargo saw, but he read experience and steadiness in each face, saw men who knew their business and had pride in that.

"Bill Alderson's agreed to your pay," Fargo said. "But he didn't know a lot of things I've found out. This won't be just a hard job. This could be the last job for any of us. I want to level with you. There'll be trouble, and a lot of it. The French want those Arabians, a rebel named Álvarez wants them, and the Comanche will try for them. Could be others, too. I'm picking up a good bit of gold due me, enough to triple what Bill Alderson agreed to pay each of you. But you might still want out. Think about it for a day."

"I don't need to think on it," Tom Bessie said. "Triple pay is all I have to hear. That's worth a little fighting any day."

"Same for me," a man named Karl Holst agreed. The others held back answering.

"All those going meet me in two days at the Consaldo-López ranch. Sam knows where it is," Fargo said. "If I'm not there, you'll know I got unlucky."

He left, rode unhurriedly back toward the Rio Grande, crossed the river as dark slid over the land. He'd already formed plans. Álvarez would have his rocks crawling with sentries. Trying to get past all of them would be pretty damn hard. He'd go in first up front. Álvarez would hold to his own set of twisted principles. He'd kill a man, but he wouldn't cheat him. Fargo made a small, wry sound. He had to make sure Álvarez kept to that. He quickened the Ovaro's pace as he rode toward the distant rock-bound mountains.

The moon hung high when he reached the base of the rocks, more than enough light for him to find his way. He grunted in satisfaction. The moon would give light for seeing and deep shadows for hiding. He started up into the rock mountains, found the three giant saguaro cactus, and turned up the pathway, turned off again at the heavy growth of yucca. He was moving easily into the center of the rocks when he saw a figure appear on horseback, blocking the pathway. He glimpsed a second man, rifle in hand, atop a flat rock.

"*¡Pare!*" the rider said.

Fargo halted, saw the second horseman move toward him from the other side.

"Álvarez expects me," Fargo called.

The two horsemen came closer, exchanged words, and Fargo saw that one recognized him. The man beckoned and Fargo swung in behind him and followed as the second sentry returned to the flat rock. The man led the way and Fargo noted that the sentries dotting the rocks on both sides lowered their rifles when his guide uttered a short whistle. He had counted eight sentries by the time he was led across the flat plateau and through the deep passage in the rocks. Another sentry guarded the exit of the passage that opened onto the camp. Fargo's glance swept the area, saw most of the men seated around a kettle on a fire. A few rose as he watched, their meal ended.

He scanned the area again. Isabel was not in sight, but the tent was closed, he saw.

The sentry motioned for Fargo to dismount and strode to the tent as the other man kept his rifle trained on the intruder. Fargo saw the tent flap open and Álvarez came out, the man's face grim and drawn tight. "You could have been shot, Fargo," he said. "Coming up here at night is a foolish act."

"Want my ten percent," Fargo said. "I'm pulling out."

Álvarez peered at him. "I did not expect you so soon," the man said.

"I told you, I'm pulling out," Fargo said.

"You did your work well for me," Álvarez said. Fargo saw the man continue to study him. "You have been at the Consaldo ranch?" he asked.

"Not since I sent María to you. I'm not much welcome there," Fargo said. "You've my gold?" he asked brusquely.

"Wait here," Álvarez said, and walked back to the tent. Fargo let a sigh escape him. The rebel leader had accepted the fact he had just come for his pay. Fargo waited and Álvarez emerged from the tent with two small but heavy sacks. "Ten percent, a little more or less. Still a lot of gold. It will bring many *americano* dollars to you," the man said.

Fargo took the sacks, walked to the Ovara, and put them into his saddlebag. He pulled himself onto the Ovaro and, as he did so, let his glance sweep the camp again. Most of the men were already settling down to sleep against the rock sides of the site. A few still remained at the kettle. He counted only two sentries within the area, the one at the mouth of the passageway, another near the tent. The sweeping glance that gathered in so much took but a second. "*Adiós,*" he said.

The rebel leader's harsh, unsmiling face didn't change.

"*Adiós*," he echoed, turned away, and barked commands at his sentry. "See him out of the mountains," he said.

The sentry moved his mount through the opening in the rocks and Fargo followed, staying close on the man's heels. He emerged at the other end of the passageway onto the flat rock table, followed the sentry as he scanned the rocks. He spotted another horseman watch them cross the flatland and move into another passageway of rocky walls. The passage led downward, widened, and Fargo saw the deep black shadows that meant that there were side passages opening from the main one. A ledge of rock jutted far out over the passageway, shutting out the sky.

Fargo halted the Ovaro and the other man turned at once. Fargo dismounted, knelt, and picked up the Ovaro's right forefoot. The sentry guiding him halted, barked a command in Spanish. Fargo held the Ovaro's forefoot from the ground and pointed to the ankle. The sentry backed his horse, turned, and came over to him, and swung down to the ground.

Fargo continued to hold the Ovaro's forefoot up, as if waiting for the man to look at it. The rebel sentry started to bend to examine the ankle, and Fargo, every muscle tensed, smashed a blow into the man's jaw, leapt as he did so. He heard the crack of a jawbone as the sentry sank, his rifle falling from his hands. Fargo caught the rifle before it could clatter against the rocks and let the man collapse in a soft heap. He pulled the figure into one of the pitch-black side passages and examined the man again. Satisfied he'd be unconscious for most of the night, he took his pistol, rifle, and bowie knife, stuffed the knife and pistol in his waist and the rifle alongside his Sharps in the saddle holster. He led the Ovaro by the reins, turned back up the passageway, and halted just before it emerged onto the plateau. He crept to the very edge, knelt down, and searched the rocks above. The sentry came into view again a few minutes later, astride his horse. Fargo watched, followed the man's movements, waited, continued to watch until he was satisfied. The sentry had a pattern, once across the rocks to the right, once back to the left, then to the very end of his area and back to the right.

Fargo waited, watched the man slowly move to the right, start back to the left of the rocks. Fargo darted forward, a silent shadow streaking across the edge of the rocks, clambering up to where the sentry patroled, clawing with his fingers and toes at tiny crevices and protrusions. When he reached the top, the sentry had returned to the right and was circling to the back of his patrol area. Fargo drew the bowie from his belt as the sentry came toward him. The man's gaze swept over his head, out and down to the flat table below. He never saw the figure in the deep shadows, but he felt the sharp, searing pain of the bowie knife, but only for an instant as the blade cut the heart muscle when it hurtled into his chest.

Fargo watched him topple from the horse, then slowly let himself slide backward to the flat rocks below. He climbed onto the Ovaro and moved up the passageway, dismounted when he'd gone half the distance, and moved forward on foot. He neared the end of the passage through the rock wall and sank to the stones to wait.

He let another hour slowly pass away in the darkness before he finally rose and started up through the remainder of the passageway, silent steps soft as a mountain cat. The camp area came into view beyond the end of the passage, the fire out, dim, dark. He heard snoring. The men slept, but not the sentry. Two, he reminded himself as he crept forward.

Fargo reached the end of the passageway, saw the first sentry only a few feet away. The man had leaned his rifle against the rock wall, stretched, and Fargo's eyes went to the sentry outside the tent. He leaned half-asleep against a stone. Álvarez had dedicated followers but poor sentries, Fargo grunted silently. His hand reached down, stole the double-edged throwing blade from the holster at his calf. He let his glance sweep the camp. The men slept heavily, the tent flap drawn shut. He raised his arm and took aim, flung the slender blade with a quick snap of the wrist. It hissed through the night, hurtled into the man's ear, deep through to the brain until the hilt against flesh halted its thrust.

The sentry died instantly, but he seemed to come alive as his head snapped up and his body jiggled in place in what seemed a strange little dance before he slumped against the stone wall and slid to the ground. Fargo ran along the wall of stone, retrieved his slender blade, wiped it clean across the man's jacket, and ran in a crouch. He was almost at the tent when the sentry there snapped awake, heard or sensed something, blinked, started to focus when Fargo's blow smashed into him, the butt of the Colt this time. The man crumpled and Fargo caught him as he did, lowering him to the ground. He stayed crouched with the unconscious form, listened, heard only the snoring and the whinny of a horse. He rose and pulled the tent flap back. He saw light and halted, putting his eye to the tiny opening. A candle on the ground burned low; he pulled the flap wider and saw Álvarez first. The man slept, a rifle at his side. Then he found Isabel on the other side of the tent, wrists and ankles bound.

She lay on her side, but her eyes were open, staring into space. He saw them grow round in shocked surprise as he slipped into the tent. He held a finger to his lips and stepped up to her, using the slender blade to sever her wrist bonds first, then her ankles. He'd just finished when Álvarez came awake, half-turned, and sat up, his and reaching for the rifle. But the big Colt pressed into his face. The man drew back, took his hand from the rifle. He stared, consuming hatred in his black eyes, his face drawn tight. He spoke and his mouth hardly moved.

"I made a mistake about you," he said.

"You made a mistake about her," Fargo answered. "You'd no reason to take her. It was a coward's act."

"She is one of them. I used her the way they have always used others," Álvarez bit out. "You are a fool, Fargo, and soon you will be a dead fool."

"This Colt is pointing at you, not me," Fargo said.

Álvarez didn't change expression, the black eyes glittering. "You have the gun in my face but you cannot use it. One shot and you will never get out of this tent alive," he said. Fargo swore under his breath, all too aware of the truth in the man's words. "Put the gun down and maybe I will take pity on you and let you leave alive. You can spread the word that Álvarez can be a man of mercy."

"I put the gun down and I'm dead for sure," Fargo said.

Álvarez shrugged. "You are dead one way or another," he said.

"Turn around," Fargo ordered.

"You surprise me again, Fargo. I did not take you for the kind to shoot a man in the back," Álvarez said as he turned.

"Crazy bastard," Fargo muttered as he smashed the butt of the Colt onto the rebel leader's head and Álvarez crumpled to the ground. He spun, reached down, and pulled Isabel to her feet. For the first time he saw that she wore a nightdress buttoned to the neck, no shoes. The bottom of the full-length gown hung in long torn sections. She came to him, leaned against him for a moment, surprisingly warm.

"He was going to kill me," she said. "No matter what. I knew that. I felt it."

"That's why I'm here, honey," he said. He glanced a[t] Álvarez as he stepped past him, Isabel clinging to hi[s] arm. "He won't be out for long. All that hate in him wil[l] wake him up," Fargo said. "We've got to get out o[f] here."

He paused at the tent flap, peered into the moonli[t] night. The men continued to sleep heavily, the two sentries prone, lifeless figures on the ground. He moved in [a] long, loping trot, crouched over, across the center of the camp toward the passageway on the other side where the Ovaro waited. Isabel on his heels, he'd just passed nea[r] the kettle atop the glowing embers when he heard Isabel cry out. "Goddamn," he hissed, whirled on her.

"A hot piece of wood, I stepped on it," she said, and he saw the sleeping figures wake, sit up.

"Run, dammit," he growled as he raced for the passageway. He heard the shouts, sounds of men waking.

"There," someone shouted as he reached the Ovaro. A shot rang out, another chipping a piece of the stone away. He yanked Isabel onto the saddle in front of him and sent the horse racing through the passageway.

"They'll find Álvarez. They'll wake him up," Isabel said.

Fargo grunted in grim agreement as they reached the end of the passageway. He turned the Ovaro sharply and started up a slope, racing higher into the mountains.

"What are you doing? We've got to get out of here."

"Not by going down," Fargo said. "That way's full of sentries and that's the way Álvarez will figure we went. He'll come charging down after us, send his men to scour the areas between here and the base of the mountains. But we'll be going up higher." He sent the Ovaro racing up a side path, higher into the rocky fastness, brushed past a handful of windblown, misshapen trees. "By the time he realizes we're not down there, we'll be moving down the back side."

Fargo followed narrow passages that led upward and moved through the rocky heights and pinnacled peaks until the land began to drop off. They had reached the backside of the rock mountain formation and he began to follow black crevices that led downward.

He halted, let the Ovaro rest, slid from the saddle, then helped Isabel down. She moved a few paces from him, her black eyes round as she turned to him. "I know about the demands he made. He took great pleasure in telling me about them," she said. "They weren't demands. They were my death warrant."

"You don't know that," Fargo said.

"No kind words. It's too late for that," she said. "Alfredo is too weak and selfish to give up everything. He'd turn his back. I know that. And my father, he is not who I once thought he was. He has spent a lifetime avoiding the need to sacrifice for anything. He couldn't change so quickly to bring himself to make the supreme sacrifice, even if he wanted to. It would not be in him. One would turn away out of weakness, the other out of habit."

Fargo saw the harsh reality of her words echoed in her eyes as she stared out into the moonlit rock formations. Barefoot, in a torn and shredded nightgown, she somehow managed to be regal, poised, beautiful, and he felt only admiration for the strength inside her. But he heard the sudden bitterness that laced her voice as she looked at him. "And you came for me out of pity," she said. "But you came at least, and I owe you my life."

"Crap," Fargo snapped, saw her eyes flare. "I don't do things out of pity." He pulled himself onto the Ovaro as he stared at him, unmoving.

"I'd like to believe that," she said.

"Believe whatever you want. It's the truth," he growled. "Now get your ass up here."

She came and he pulled her into the saddle in front of

him, feeling the warmth of her tight little ass as sh
pressed against him. He sent the horse down a slope
rock walls on both sides. His arms reached around her a
he held the Ovaro in, and the soft sides of her breast
pushed against him. He was sorry when the slope levele
and he relaxed his hold on the reins, dropped his arm
lower. A line of pink appeared on the horizon, widened
slowly tore apart the curtain of night. "I can't make it al
the way back from here, not without rest," Isabel said
and he heard the exhaustion in her voice.

"Don't plan to keep on. I'll find a spot to hole up," h
told her. "When he doesn't find us, Álvarez will know wha
we did. He'll come down to the flatland and hope to catcl
us when we come around the base of the mountain."

"Which we'll have to do," she added.

"In our own time and way. He can't stay down fo
more than a few hours or run into a French patrol. H
can't risk that yet, not until he gets more men, which tha
gold shipment will help him do. But now he'll have t
retreat back into his mountains by noon, I'd guess."

"He's a madman, Fargo. He believes in Juárez, bu
he's a madman," Isabel said. "He won't let this go by
Fargo. He'll come for you somehow, someway."

"I expect he will," Fargo agreed, his eyes sweeping
the land below as the rocks began to stretch out, become
longer, less jagged. He swerved the pinto suddenly as he
caught a flash of blue-white, a small mountain stream
dropping over the rocks. He brought the horse through a
narrow place into a rock-lined circle where the smal
waterfall bubbled into a clear pool and the ground wa:
deep with soft lipfern, long, slender leaves layered atop
one another, soft as a feather mattress. A low rock over
hang afforded shade from the heat of the sun.

"Perfect," he said, and slid to the ground with Isabel
He led the Ovaro under the overhang, unsaddled the

horse, and watched Isabel sink down on the fern. She curled onto her side and was asleep in minutes. He lay down near her, closed his eyes, and the tiredness pulled sleep over him as though it were a blanket. Even though he lay under the rock overhang, the heat of the Mexican day drained energies, and when he woke, the sun was in the afternoon sky. His glance flicked to Isabel, found her gone, and he sat up, saw her in the nightdress but her hair wet. She dried herself with a towel he recognized as coming from his saddlebag, and she glanced up as he rose, came toward her.

"I didn't think you'd mind," she said, her onyx tresses glistening under the sun.

"Be my guest," he said. He started toward the little pool, shed his shirt.

"Wait," she said. "Answer me something. No pity, you said. Why did you come after me?"

"Had a hand in putting you there, figured I ought to try getting you out," he answered.

She nodded gravely. "Good-enough reason," she said.

"There's a better one," he said. "I hate waste, especially of anything beautiful, anything worth saving."

She pulled the towel from her hair, her eyes wide. "You always surprise one, don't you?" she said.

He tossed her a grin and walked on, shed the rest of his clothes as he reached the clear, cool little pool. He kicked off shorts as he stepped into the water. It was deep at once, deliciously cool, and he let it flow around him, wash away tiredness, grime, the burning sun. His eyes swept the little alcove. It was completely sheltered, only one way in, the way they had come.

Isabel, the nightdress open at the neck, watched him as he dived, came up, let the little waterfall gently splash over him. He swam to the edge of the little pool, reached out and took his shorts, drew them on as he emerged.

They clung instantly to the wetness of his skin, outlined every part of him as he walked toward her. He saw her black eyes on him, move down to where the shorts pressed tight over the bulge of his organ. He halted before her, sank to his knees, and her eyes lifted, stared at him. He pressed his mouth on hers and felt her lips open at once, soft sweetness, respond, press back against his. He felt the frown of surprise cross his forehead as he pulled back, peered at her.

"Been facing truth suddenly," Isabel breathed. "It's habit-forming. You can't stop."

She leaned forward, brushed his lips with hers, pulled away, and stood up. Slowly, she began to unbutton the top of the nightdress and he stayed on his knees, his eyes on her. She unbuttoned the garment to the last button at the waist, wriggled her shoulders, and the nightdress fell away, dropped down to her waist, then slid onto the ground. She stood before him, tall, lithesome, sinuous body, stood very straight, a sudden pride holding her. Her breasts were longer than they'd seemed under clothes, but gracefully long, flowing, delicate curves that rounded at the bottoms, a brown-pink nipple center on each, areolas small, deep pink. Her torso narrowed, a flat, almost inward-curved abdomen, moved in a sinuous line to fine-boned hips and a black, tangly, dense nap over the rise of her pubic mount, the most luxuriant nap he had ever seen. It seemed almost a symbol of turbulent, tangled sensuousness.

Isabel took a step backward, her head held high, eyes shining, her onyx hair falling loosely over her wide shoulders. She was reveling in his gaze, he saw, enjoying the desire and appreciation she could see in his face, as though she were suddenly totally aware of the power of her own beauty. She came forward to him, the gracefully long breasts level with his face. She cupped her hand ınder one, pushed it toward him. It would have seemed rude, perhaps coarse, from others, but from Isabel it was an offering, the priestess holding the chalice of pleasure out to the chosen. He closed his lips around the soft breast, drew it into his mouth.

"Oh . . . aaa . . . aaaaah, yes, oh, God," Isabel cried out, and she put her head back, pressed herself hard into his face. He sucked on the offering, caressed, pulled, kissed, circled the little tip with his lips, and felt its spongy softness change in his mouth, take on firmness. "Fargo, Fargo . . ." Isabel breathed, and he pulled his mouth from her breasts. She arched backward, seemed to hang suspended, the black hair falling long and loose. He brought her forward, pulled her down to him, and she fell back onto the cool, soft cover of fern that blanketed the little alcove. Her black eyes held deep fires and she stared as though she did not completely believe her own actions. Her arms came up, circled his neck, pulled his head down to her breasts, and again she cried out at the touch of his lips, his tongue.

The long, lovely thighs pressed together as he lay his body over hers, his maleness pounding as it touched against her abdomen. "No . . . oh, oh, God . . ." she half-screamed, and he felt the tenseness of her legs as she held them tight together. He pulled his mouth from her breasts, found her lips, kissed her, let his tongue slip inside her mouth. She murmured, half-groaned, pleasure in each sound, and his hand moved down across her breasts, cradled and stroked and cupped each, moved slowly along her narrow waist, traced a fevered path downward, circled the dark little hole in the center of her belly, went on. He found the small rise, felt the edges of the black tangled filaments of hair, pushed his fingers into the deep denseness, and pressed, felt the softly rounded curve of her little mound underneath.

135

Her hands fluttered up and down his back, and he fel her tongue suddenly dart at him, thrust forward, tiny sudden motions. Her legs remained pressed togethe and he felt the pull of her thigh muscles. He let his fin gers slip downward, over the curve at the end of the tan gled nap, and he felt the heat, wet, flowing hotness "No," he heard her murmur. "No, Fargo . . . oh, ol . . ." He pressed deeper, his finger pushing down, swee searching, and the trembling came through her body, a sudden spasm. He pressed further, gently, the tip of hi finger suddenly touching the soft wet lips. Her stomach sucked in and she seemed to stop breathing for ar instant, and then he heard her cry, a long, low wailing sound, half-surrender, half-acceptance. Her long leg came apart, the slender thighs falling open. "Yes, ye . . . Fargo, please, now, now," she breathed. "Now, now, now."

Her hands moved up and down across his back, his chest, and he let his fingers push against the warm wetness of her and she cried out. She pushed and his hand moved deeper, touching, stroking. "Oh, my God . . . oh, Jesus, oh, oh, oh . . . eeee . . . eeeee . . ." Isabel half-screamed. He felt the long thighs close, trapping his fingers inside her, and her legs pressed hard together as if to ensure against his leaving. He stroked again inside her and she pressed her hips downward as her legs fell open again. He moved, brought his throbbing gift over the tangled dense brush, pulled it downward, pressed forward, found the dark portal. He slid forward slowly as the tightness of her closed around him. He halted and she clutched at him. "Go on . . . go on," she screamed. He pushed, slowly, heard the tiny cries come from her, half-pain, half-anticipation. They continued, rose higher as he slipped deeper and then, suddenly, thrust hard and felt her tightness tear loose.

"Oooooooh . . . iiiiaaaaaa . . . oh, Fargo, oh, Fargo," Isabel screamed, and the pain was filled with pleasure, the pleasure laced with pain. He started to slowly draw back, but her hands dug into him. "No, no . . . more, more, oh, God more," she screamed. He moved in again, began to slide back and forth, found the slow rhythm that matched her gasped breaths. Her hands cupped the long breasts, pushed them upward for him, and he buried his face against her, took one rounded softness into his mouth, sucked in rhythm to his slow thrustings.

Isabel cried out, each cry louder, more intense, and he felt her arms tightening, her body beginning to tremble. She dug fingers into his back and he felt her legs lift, come in against his sides. She pushed with his every stroke, lifting to meet him, falling back, pushing forward again. She learned quickly, the fire burning high, and he was deep inside her when he felt her hands pause, curl against him, and her pubic mound lifted. Little sounds came from her, gasps, one upon the other. "Oh, oh, oh . . . oh, oh . . . oh, God," Isabel cried out. "It's happening . . . it's happening."

He drew back, held, waited, and felt her wetness spill hard from her, her long legs lift as she dug heels into the ground. He thrust deep and hard, furiously exploding with her as her scream tore at the rock walls, echoed, reverberated, and her entire torso shook with violent tremors. Her scream ended, an abrupt silence, and once again she seemed to stop breathing. She hung with him, heels still dug into the ground, and he saw her black eyes staring at him, almost a disbelief in their deep orbs. Slowly, she let herself go, slide backward to the ground. "No . . . no," she whispered. "So quick . . . so quick." She lay beneath him and the disbelief had become protest. "Not enough," she murmured. "Not enough."

137

"It never is." He smiled gently at her, drew from her, and rolled over to lay beside her. She turned her face to him, her eyes all deep softness. "First time, wasn't it?" he said, and she nodded, lay against him for another moment, then rose onto her elbow, and he watched one long breast fall gracefully to the side and touch against his chest.

"Not enough," she murmured, and pulled herself straighter. She took both hands, began to run them up and down his body, coming close to his waiting maleness, moving again, each long caressing massage stronger, pressing harder against him. He felt the excitement spiraling inside him, desire and power returning, lifting his maleness, proclaiming its eager readiness. He heard Isabel gasp little breaths, saw her staring at him, and then she fell upon him, her hands curled around him, stroking, caressing, rubbing her flat belly against him, and she suddenly cried out, pulled at him as she rolled onto her back. She dug heels into the ground again, lifted herself for him, thighs pulled wide. "Fargo, Fargo, come to me, Fargo . . . come, come," she called, urgent, desperate pleas. He pulled himself over her and slid inside her, and she began to pump at once, no waiting, no holding back, no hesitant fears now, and he saw her lips drawn back in a smile as she pumped with him, pushed, drew back, cried out in joy, and held him tight into her as she locked her arms around him.

When the moment came again, her scream rose higher than before, hung in the air as she did, clung to the peak of ecstasy, and once more the cry was cut off abruptly in the silence that he realized now was pure protest, unwillingness to accept the evanescence of ecstasy. She rolled against him, curled up in his arms, her jet hair a black halo around the finely modeled beauty of her face. She half-dozed with him and he snapped his eyes open as he felt her get up after a little while.

She stepped into the sun, magnificently tall, the sinuousness of her body awesomely beautiful as she walked to the pool, plunged in, dived, came up, and pulled herself out. She walked back to where he lay, the sun bringing out the faint olive tint to her skin, little glistening drops of water clinging to her. She knelt, pressed herself over him, and the coolness of her skin penetrated his warmth, soothing, stimulating, contrasts that seemed to work. She lay on him, not moving for a long time, drinking in the tactile pleasure of flesh upon flesh. He felt her move finally, after he'd closed his eyes, slowly rub the thick luxuriant tangle back and forth across his organ.

He opened his eyes, saw a delicious little smile edging her lips. "Isabel Teresa Concepción, you've no right to a name like that," he said. "You're a damn wanton."

"Yes," she said happily.

He laughed with her and loved with her again, and they lay exhausted as the sun slipped down over the rocks.

"Time we moved on," he said finally.

She nodded, stretched, reached over and pulled the nightdress over herself, buttoned it up and managed to look instantly proper. He rose and she came to him, leaned against him as he started to pull on clothes. "It was wonderful, more wonderful than I'd ever dreamed. You made it so," she said. "You made me come alive, feel, know."

"Would've come to you sooner or later," he said.

"No, not like this. You understand the senses, you know from inside," she said, pressed herself against him, and finally stepped back. "You understood me from the very first," she said as he finished dressing. The dusk slipped into night as he saddled the Ovaro, pulled the cinch tight. "You'll be staying at the ranch from now on, with me," she said.

"Can't," he said.

"Because of Alfredo and my father? I'll see to them," Isabel said grimly.

"Because I'll be heading back tomorrow with the Arabians," he said, and saw her eyes grow wide.

She stared at him, the tiny frown of disbelief digging deeper into her forehead. "No," she breathed. "You don't mean that. You can't, not after today."

"Today's got nothing to do with it," he said.

"Today has everything to do with it." She frowned.

"You do it for that?" he asked. "You do it just to convince me to leave the horses?"

"No, of course not, never," she protested. "But something happened between us. It is different now."

"Different, but not that different," he said.

"I don't understand this, I don't understand you," she threw back. "You make love to me like a saint and now you are a monster. How can you change so?"

"Didn't change any," he said.

But the hurt and the anger kept spiraling inside her, he saw, her eyes black fire. "None of it was for me, was it? You came after me because of your own conscience, and then you took your reward. That's all you really wanted. I understand it now," she flung at him.

"You understand nothing," he tossed back. "There's right and there's wrong and there's your little beaver, and they don't hang together, none of them, much as you'd like it that way."

Her voice sobbed a curse as she flew at him. "Damn you, Fargo," she said, fists clenched, trying to rain blows on him. He stepped aside, grasped her arm, and spun her around, sent her half-falling, half-stumbling. He was at her when she turned, pulled her to him, and she leaned into his chest, the fight abruptly gone. "You don't understand, you don't," she half-sobbed.

140

"You've an obsession with this thing," he told her. "I'm only taking the horses Bill Alderson bought. You'll have half a stable left, some of the best of your stock, I'm sure."

"It's not just that. It's all of it. I told you I won't have them ruined," she said. "I raised most of those young ones."

"And I told you Bill Alderson's not that kind," he snapped. "Now get in the saddle. I'm not talking more about it with you. I've a job to do and I'm going to do it." He turned, pulled himself onto the Ovaro, and helped her climb up in front of him. She leaned back against him, head almost on his shoulder as he walked the horse down to the bottom of the rocks and onto the dry flatland.

The night stayed warm and the moon came up to light the delicate planes of her lovely face. He rode slowly, let the pinto make its own way across the terrain, and the moon had climbed high when they reached the line of black persimmon trees.

"Rein up," Isabel said, and he pulled the horse to a halt. She slid from the saddle, turned to peer up at him. "You said there's right and there's wrong and there is our making love and they're separate," she slid at him.

"Close enough," he agreed.

"Then make love to me one more time, here, now," Isabel said. "Make me know it once more, before the world comes apart."

"You think that's what's going to happen?" Fargo asked, and she nodded, unsmiling.

"One more time, for today, for tomorrow, for remembering," he said. Her black eyes beckoned, dark fires smolding.

He swung from the saddle, pulled his bedroll down, tossed it on the ground. She was atop it, the nightdress flung aside, waiting catlike for him as he shed clothes.

"Damn you, Fargo," she hissed as he came to her, and she pressed the long breasts into his face, moved her body to find his mouth. She made love with a breathless, almost angry urgency, demanding harshness from him, her fingers digging into his back as she pushed against him, with him, her body a weapon of pleasure until finally her scream spiraled into the night, no abrupt ending this time but a half-sob, half-groan that became a hoarse whisper, and she rolled over to lay beside him, deep breaths gasping in air.

She sat up after a few minutes and in the black eyes he saw the fire and ice again, equal parts of each, but the cool, contained control had something new in it, a terrible bitterness that gave her aristocratic face the edge of hardness. She pulled the nightdress on as he donned clothes, strapped his gun belt on, and she was waiting on the Ovaro when he swung into the saddle. She rode the rest of the way to the ranch in silence, and Fargo saw the tall front door of the house open as the Ovaro's hooves echoed on the hard ground. He dismounted, swung Isabel down beside him as Don Miguel and Alfredo rushed from the house.

Isabel took a step forward and Don Miguel rushed at her, arms outstretched to embrace her when he halted, his thin lips parting as he stared at his daughter.

"Isabel, my child," he said, and Fargo saw the cold pits that were Isabel's eyes. "You are safe, thank God, thank God," Don Miguel said. He stayed back, at arm's length, held there by the invisible but very real wall Isabel had flung at him. "María told us Fargo went to try and save you. We could do nothing but wait and pray. We died a thousand deaths, my child," the man said.

"I almost died one," Isabel said, each word sheathed in ice.

"We were afraid to do the wrong thing," Alfredo said. "We wanted to do what was best."

"Best for whom?" Isabel hissed.

"We did not know what to do. You shouldn't be angry with us," Alfredo protested.

"I have no anger," Isabel said, her glance going from one to the other. "Only contempt and disgust." She turned to the big man beside her, and the fire and ice stayed in her eyes, but they came together for an instant, a warm, smoldering liquid. She pressed her lips to him, lingered, finally pulled back.

"You won't be here when I come back tomorrow, will you?" he said.

"No," she answered softly. He nodded, words unnecessary. "I will remember everything you have taught me," she said. "Everything." She turned, walked into the house, ignored Alfredo and Don Miguel with utter disdain as she brushed past them.

Fargo remounted, rode away with equal disdain, his eyes narrowed in thought. Isabel's words rode with him. On the surface, they had meant all that had passed between them, and yet he felt something more, the unsaid again. He tabled his thoughts as he rode north, crossed the Rio Grande under the moon, and reached Sam Alderson's spread just as the man was about to turn down the last lamp.

"Thought you were meeting the boys at the Consaldo place," Alderson said in surprise.

"Slight change in plans," Fargo said. "Tell you, come morning."

The man nodded, gestured to a cot in the side room, and Fargo shed his clothes and stretched out wearily. He went to sleep with visions of long, soft breasts and things that were unfinished.

7

Morning dawned dry and hot. They were all there, eight of them, no one cutting out, and Fargo was grateful for that. He took the two sacks of gold, spilled them out on Sam Alderson's table. The gold pieces were each worth a year's pay or more.

"Triple pay in advance," Fargo said. These men were not the kind to let up because they had pay in hand. "Someone gets sidetracked, has to hole up, he'll have a full kick when he gets loose."

"Fair enough," Tom Bessie said as each man took his share.

Fargo turned to Alderson. "I need fifteen or twenty old nags. Don't care what they're like. Know where I can get them?" he asked.

Alderson answered at once. "Ollie Oldenkamp over in Bellsville. He's always got a couple dozen old plugs. He sells and swaps them to place miners, snake-oil salesmen, and the like. He'll be happy as a pig in mud to unload all you'll take."

"Let's get them," Fargo said, and strode from the house. The wranglers followed and he rode among them as they headed for the town Alderson had mentioned, northwest of Laredo and behind a rise in the land. "We'll have to get the Arabians past the French first. They keep a constant patrol and we'll be in their backyard," Fargo explained. "Our only chance is to move them out by night."

"The French don't patrol then?" Karl Holst asked.

"They'll be camped, watching. They've a Major Andrade. He's smart enough to figure I might try to move the Arabians by dark," Fargo said.

"So why the old nags we're going to get?" a wrangler named Johnston asked.

"We're going to make decoys out of them, let the French chase us while we slip the Arabians across the border," Fargo said.

He saw Tom Bessie smile, Slim Staunton follow with a laugh. "I like it," Bessie said. "We'll make it work."

"First we've got to bring the nags in. We'll take turns, bring them in two at a time, nice and easy. Nobody's going to pay any mind to a man with two old plugs. We'll ease them into the stables at the Consaldo ranch," Fargo said as they came in sight of the slightly run-down spread, the collection of horses in the pens unmistakably marking it as the right place.

Fargo made the purchase quickly, disdained any bargaining, and his wranglers led the horses back toward the border territory. Fargo halted a half-mile short of the river. "I'll bring the first two over, you take the next two, Karl," he said. "The Consaldo ranch is due south. You'll see it plain enough when you get near." He gathered the rope halters on an old bay and a chunky mare and moved casually toward the riverbank, crossed into Mexico, and made his way slowly toward the ranch. He put the two horses in the first corral and saw Don Miguel walking toward him.

"You will be taking the Arabians now?" the man asked.

"Not for a while. My boys are bringing in some extra horses for the trip," Fargo said casually. His eyes moved past the man, sought the elegant surrey, and saw it was not outside the house in its usual spot. "Isabel take the surrey?" he asked.

"No, she left early, before I could talk to her. Alfredo took it on business," Don Miguel said. "You have the check for me, *señor?*" the man asked, his voice cold, distaste in each word.

Fargo drew Bill Alderson's check from an inside shirt pocket and handed it to the man. Don Miguel examined it, put it into a flat wallet, fastened the big man with a cold glance. "You have turned out to be a very difficult man, *señor*," he said.

"You have turned out to be a real shit," Fargo said.

Don Miguel's aristocratic face stiffened and he spun on his heel and strode away.

Fargo leaned back against the corral fence, straightened as he saw María come from the clay hut and hurry toward him. She halted before him, wore the scoop-neck white blouse she had on the first time he'd seen her. Her eyes were deep with concern.

"Leave as soon as you can, Fargo," she said. "Alfredo went to the French. I heard him tell Don Miguel."

Fargo smiled, ran his hand across her face. "I figured that," he said. "He's striking back in his coward's way, staying on the right side of his French masters."

"He will tell them you are taking the Arabians today. They will be waiting, watching," she said.

"Figured that, too," Fargo said, and saw a tiny frown touch María's face.

"But it is not the French I come to warn you about," she said. "It is Álvarez. He has sworn to kill you. You will never take the Arabians back to America, he has said."

"I'll get a good start. He doesn't know I'm moving them out today," Fargo said.

Her face stayed grave. "He will know. He has eyes all

146

ver. He has sent men across the border already, waiting, watching. Believe me, Fargo," María said.

Fargo took her words in, grimaced. They were probably all too true. Unlike the French, Álvarez wouldn't hesitate about going deep into the Texas territory.

"I'll stay ready for him," he told her. "Thanks for telling me. Makes us even."

"I'll be in the house all day," she said, her deep-brown eyes taking on tiny lights.

His smile was rueful. "It'd be nice," he said. "Maybe, I can find time."

"*Vaya con Dios*," she said softly, and he watched her return to the little clay house, soft round rear moving provocatively, her earthy sexuality trailing after. He saw Karl Holst riding up with the next two horses and tossed away the thoughts that had started to nibble at him.

"Slim's on the way," Karl told him as they corralled the horses with the first two. Karl returned to pick up others and Fargo stayed, helping Slim Staunton when he arrived. The entire operation didn't finish till the day was almost over. Don Miguel had stopped by at one point and frowned at the horses in the corral.

"Back-up mounts," Fargo said cheerfully, and the man walked on. When the last of the horses arrived, Fargo called Pedro, the short-legged ranch manager. "Turn out the Arabians," he said. "My boys will take it from there."

The man nodded and went into the stable. Moments later the Arabians raced into the training ring and Fargo saw the wranglers gather by the fence at once, their experienced eyes taking in the steeds.

"Never saw the likes of them," a man named Synder said, awe in his voice.

"They'll take a heap of handling," Slim Staunton observed.

"Don't push them, don't stay too tight on them," Tom

Bessie said, thinking aloud. "Herd them but give 'e∎ space and they'll handle all right."

Fargo watched the night sliding over the flatlan∎ beyond the ranch. "Saw a half-dozen French soldie∎ moving down to the Rio Grande," one of the wrangle∎ told him.

"The rest are probably there by now," Fargo sai∎ "The major will expect I'll be crossing there at th∎ narrowest spot. He'll be waiting with his *chasseurs*." H∎ paused, set his thoughts in order as the others waite∎ "Tom and I will take the old nags. They won't take muc∎ handling. The rest of you take the Arabians. Put rop∎ halters on a couple to be sure they go along close, and th∎ rest you can ride herd. Head north, parallel the rive∎ Keep on a half-mile or so before you take them across."

"Meanwhile, you and Tom will be leading the Frenc∎ on a right nice chase downriver," Slim said.

"You've got it," Fargo answered. "One thing mor∎ very important. You take the Arabians slow, quiet as yo∎ can till you get far enough away. We'll make the noise.∎ He waited as the wranglers brought their horses into th∎ training ring, let the high-strung Arabians get used to th∎ other mounts. They put rope halters on four of the Arab∎ ans as they moved slowly among them, let them get use∎ to their voices as well. Good men, experienced men∎ Fargo grunted. He'd need every bit of their horse sens∎ to make it back. He swung onto the Ovaro and rode int∎ the adjoining corral with Tom Bessie.

"See you in Texas," he called softly, and watched th∎ Arabians as they were led out of the training ring. Th∎ men followed Tom Bessie's advice, rode herd but gav∎ the high-spirited steeds plenty of room. Fargo watche∎ the Arabians recede into the night and led the old horse∎ out of the corral, Tom Bessie taking up the rear. H∎ turned north, straight for the Rio Grande. The moon wa∎

148

new, he saw in satisfaction. The major would hear them first, but the almost black night would let him only see the horses being raced through the darkness. That was the idea, anyway, he reminded himself, quickened the Ovaro into a trot, and saw the horses follow.

He rode on another half-mile, peering into the night. The river had to be close. He raised his arm, halted, waited for the horses to settle down enough for him to strain his ears. He caught the faint sound of metal on metal, the faint clank of a bit. He turned, dimly saw Tom Bessie's form at the end of the pack. "Now," he called. "Run them hard."

He let out a shout, snapped the reins, and sent the Ovaro into a full gallop. He heard Tom whistle a whip over the horses at the rear, and the pack was racing through the night in seconds. Fargo stayed straight, headed toward the river until he glimpsed the line of figures directly in front of them. He slowed the Ovaro, came in alongside the lead horses, and turned them downriver. The others swung after them, Tom Bessie pushing them on. Fargo glanced across and saw the French troopers start to move and come together in a column.

Major Andrade's shout carried clearly. *"Prends-les . . . prends-les,"* he ordered his troops.

Fargo kept the pace, aware the old horses would slow too soon. But it was working, the French chasing hard, still unable to see more than the racing pack of horses. He angled the pack toward the river, turned them slowly. The French were closing fast, he saw. They'd be close enough to see in a few minutes. Fargo swung the lead horses again, headed more directly for the river. It would shorten the distance for the French, but it didn't matter much now. The Arabians were well on their way.

Fargo glanced to his left, saw Major Andrade leading his *chasseurs* at a full gallop. The old horses were slowing

149

fast, he saw. They'd halt by themselves damn soon, he knew. There was no driving an old horse with the wind gone out of him. He cast another glance at the French, saw the major had come well within sight of the pack. Fargo waved an arm at Tom Bessie, pointed to the river only a few dozen yards ahead, and saw Tom cut away from the rear of the pack and spur his horse forward. Fargo let the Ovaro go full out as the old horses began to falter, start to halt. He saw Major Andrade rein up, heard the man shout a curse in French, then a stream of curses. The Ovaro plunged into the river, splashed water high, and he heard Tom Bessie on his heels. Fargo reached just past midriver before he slowed, rode on a few yards farther till he felt the Ovaro's feet find the gentle slope of the bank. He halted then, turned to face across the river. The French were milling around the pack of old horses that had come to a halt, their angry shouts clearly carrying through the night. He saw one figure detach itself from the others, advance to the water's edge. He didn't need to see the major's tight face to know who it was.

"Don't say I never gave you anything," Fargo called.

"Very clever, M'sieu Fargo," Major Andrade said, the bitter anger tight in his voice. "I underestimated you."

"It's been done before," Fargo said.

"You would be foolish to set foot in Mexico again," the major said. "France will rule Mexico one day soon."

"Maybe," Fargo said.

"Absolutely," the major said.

"I wouldn't plan on retiring there," Fargo said. "You take good care of those horses, now. They might be worth a lot of money."

He wheeled the pinto and felt the major's eyes still on him as he rode onto Texas soil. He headed north with Tom Bessie riding beside him.

"Easy as pie," he heard Tom say, chuckling.

"Don't start counting chickens," Fargo growled, sent the Ovaro into a fast trot. He came into sight of the Arabians north of Laredo, let the men congratulate each other, and turned the group north, found a spot to make camp with a wall of sandstone at one side. They made a loose rope corral with stakes and lariats for the Arabians, bedded down, and Fargo decided against posting sentries for the night. He slept at once and the night passed quietly. One of the wranglers, Art Silver, had good strong coffee made when he woke, and he sipped the brew as the others gathered together.

"The Mexican won't hold back at crossing the border," Fargo told them.

"This Álvarez honcho?" Karl Holst said.

Fargo nodded. "No sense in tiring the horses by trying to move fast. We just ride and keep our eyes open," he said, finished the coffee, and rose. He let his eyes move over the terrain as the others took the rope corral down and let the Arabians stretch their legs, graze on a patch of grama grass. Nothing moved behind them across the flatland and his glance traveled along the higher ground dotted with clusters of cedar elm. He saw nothing and turned away unsatisifed, climbed onto the Ovaro, and led the herd north.

The men spread out, keeping the Arabians in a loose pocket that let the high-spirited, beautiful steeds run free. The day wore on and Fargo called a halt just after noon where a trickle of a stream ambled over the ground, providing just enough for the horses to slake their thirst without overdrinking. When he moved on, his eyes swept the land again and saw only a condor lazily circling over a line of trees. The faint purple of dusk had begun to drift toward them from the horizon when Tom Bessie trotted up to ride beside him.

"We've gone on a fair piece. I think the Mexican has called off coming after you," Tom said.

"Álvarez would figure we'll think that," Fargo muttered.

"Maybe you're giving him more than his due," Tom suggested.

"Maybe I'm not giving him enough. I haven't figured how and where he's going to come at us," Fargo said. "He's crazy and he's smart and he's got a mission. He'll come."

Tom Bessie fell silent and dropped back to the others. Then Fargo's gaze grew sharp as he saw prints on the ground, unshod hoofprints, eight ponies, he counted as he rode. The prints veered off to where the land rose, thick with greenbriars and rocks.

"Apache?" he heard Slim Staunton ask as the man watched his eyes follow the hoofprints.

Fargo nodded. "We're in their backyard," he said as he peered forward through the thickening dusk. The Apache had plenty of time to raid. Álvarez was running out of time. The deeper he let the horses go into Texas, the harder he'd have it bringing them back to Mexico. The man had delayed making his move for some reason. Fargo grimaced and felt grim uneasiness jabbing him in the pit of his stomach. His eyes strained, focused on a rock formation that rose up from the land, standing free, with the front section a large half-circle.

"That's camp for the night," he shouted to the others. "It'll give us a nice wall at our backs." He rode on ahead, dismounted, and scanned the circular sector of the rock, saw a series of ledges in what had seemed a smooth face from a distance. His lips were still pursed in thought as the others arrived with the horses, stretched lariats across the front of the half-circle, and used the stakes to make a large rope corral that gave the Arabians plenty of room. One of the men gathered brush for a small fire and broke out a can of beans to go with warmed jerky. They relaxed and exchanged the small talk of men who had spent most of their lives on the range.

Fargo rose to stare into the night, the moon still only a thin crescent in the sky. Álvarez was out there, he swore silently. He knew it, felt it in the pit of his stomach. He'd strike before the night ended, Fargo was certain. But he'd have to make a direct frontal assault if he did, the circular wall of rock protecting the rear of the camp. It'd be costly, too costly. Álvarez was too wily to risk that. Unless he felt he had no other choice. No, Fargo reconsidered silently; Álvarez would find another choice. He turned back to where the fire had burned to embers and the men were starting to get out bedrolls.

"Put 'em away," he said softly. The men turned to stare at him. "We'll be having company. I want to be ready," he said.

"Fargo, we haven't seen so much as a jackrabbit all day," Karl Holst said.

"You wouldn't see me, either, if I were watching you," Fargo snapped.

"Let him come. We've got a good position here, a solid wall at our backs. He'll have to come head-on. We'll cut him to pieces," Tom Bessie said.

"Figured the same thing. That's why I'm worried," Fargo said. "I know the man. He won't let that happen. He's got something up his sleeve. He wants those Arabians alive and he wants me dead, and he aims to get both."

"Can't see that we've any choice but to stay here and wait," Art Silver said.

"Not good enough of a choice," Fargo answered. "I'll stay here. I want him to think we're here firing back. The rest of you go around back of this rock. It stretches out far

153

enough so that if you're at both ends you'll be able to pour lead from both sides. You take up positions and wait. You'll hear him when he comes and you can catch him in a cross fire."

"Why, when we can stay here and catch him head-on?" Tom Bessie said.

Fargo shook his head. "I told you, he's not going to just run into a buzz saw. He's too smart for that."

Tom shrugged. "You're the boss. You had the Frenchmen figured. I'll go along with you," he said.

"Thanks," Fargo said. "I don't see he's close enough yet. It's a pretty dark night. But just to make sure, you slip out of here one by one, go around the back and wait."

"I'll go first," Tom Bessie said. Leading his horse behind him, he lifted the lariat forming the rope corral and edged his way along the half-circle of rock, slipped around the corner, and disappeared. The others followed, moving along to both ends until Fargo stood alone. He took the big Sharps from his saddle holster and made his way up to the first narrow ledge in the half-circle of rock some ten feet above the ground. The elevation gave him a better view of the dark flatland that stretched out before him. He lay the Sharps on the ledge, put the Colt .45 beside it, and sat back.

The slender crescent of a moon traveled slowly across the black velvet cloth that was the sky, and the night was still. Time dragged with maddening slowness, but he stayed motionless as a frog on a lily pad, his eyes staring into the darkness.

The moon had reached the center of the sky when Fargo blinked. Something moved at the very edge of the blackness. He strained his eyes, saw the movement again. It widened and the darkness took on shapes, forms, became a line of horsemen advancing at a walk. Fargo's eyes narrowed as he realized why Álvarez had delayed his move. His new gold had bought him added recruits. Fargo counted twenty-five in all. He felt his frown deepening.

Álvarez continued to advance head-on, riders and horses taking on individual shapes. It didn't make sense, and suddenly Fargo felt the oath well up in his throat. Álvarez raised one arm, something in his hand, and Fargo peered hard and the curse exploded into the air. "Son of a bitch!" he swore just as the row of horsemen burst into light, each setting fire to a torch of dry brush.

The riders exploded into a full gallop at the same instant, hidden behind their flaming torches. The long line came together as they converged on their target. Fargo heard the rifle fire from behind the torches, bullets slamming into the rock and the ground. He began to fire back, using the Sharps with one hand, the Colt with the other. He saw two of the torches drop away, fired another volley, and another torch skittered into the night. But Álvarez and his attackers had almost reached the rocks when Fargo saw them wheel, fling the dry-brush torches into the half-circle. The spiraling cascade of flame had the effect Álvarez wanted, and Fargo saw the terrified Arabians bolt in panic, trample the flimsy rope barrier as they raced from the half-circle.

Álvarez directed his riders to go after the panicked horses, but the night erupted with a new explosion of rifle fire, a deadly fusillade of cross fire that cut down ten riders with the first volley. Fargo saw Álvarez wheel his horse in surprise, duck low in the saddle. The rebel leader screamed at his Juaristas and the men tried to flee, but the cross fire poured into them and Fargo saw at least six more topple out of their saddles. He leapt to his feet, raced from the ledge as he reloaded the Colt and vaulted onto the Ovaro. Crouched low in the saddle, he roared from the half-circle, his eyes searching the fleeing figures. He found Álvarez, the man shouting commands, trying to rally his men. Most were racing into the safety of the darkness, none trying to round up the Arabians. Fargo headed the Ovaro for Álvarez, saw the man half-turn, see him coming, wheel his horse, and streak for a line of tall brush.

Fargo followed, the pinto closing the distance quickly. He saw Álvarez race through the brush, suddenly leap from his horse to disappear into the high cover. Fargo dropped half over the side of the Ovaro as the shot flew over his head instantly. He plunged into the brush and stayed hidden alongside the horse, tensed his muscles and let himself drop. He landed on his shoulders, rolled, grateful for the cushioned impact of the underbrush. He rolled again, lay still, and heard another shot whistle over his head. The brush crackled as Álvarez came through it in a crouching run, head kept below the top of the brush. Fargo lifted himself to one knee and fired just as Álvarez flung himself flat. He knew the shot missed and he dived sideways as Álvarez sent a bullet through the brush. Fargo pulled himself to one knee. The man was close, directly ahead of him, rushing through the tall brush like a wild boar. Fargo saw the dark bulk of him appear in the thick brush, dropped, and rolled as the rebel leader fired a volley of shots. Fargo heard two bullets crack through the dry brush alongside his head.

The rebel leader's form exploded through the brush, his arm upraised, an eight-inch blade in his hand. The man's mad hate gave him not only a consuming fury but a kind of protection, a complete disregard for his own life that propelled him beyond the actions of normal men. The man leapt through the air like a puma, the knife upraised, and Fargo managed to half-roll, feeling the knife slice through the back of his shirt. He rolled again, brought the Colt up as Álvarez, eyes glittering with wild hatred, flung the blade. Once again, Fargo had to twist away, just managing to flatten himself enough so the blade brushed only the back of his neck. He rolled onto his back as Álvarez dived for him, both hands outstretched. Fargo's finger squeezed back on the trigger and he heard the hammer click on an empty chamber.

Álvarez uttered a cry of mad triumph and Fargo got one arm up as the man landed on him, catching him in the throat with his forearm. Álvarez gagged, fell to one side, gagged again as Fargo rolled away, started to get to his feet. The man, his mouth open to draw in breath, his face contorted with pain, dived into the brush, and Fargo saw his hand close around the knife. Álvarez started to turn and bring his arm up, but Fargo stepped in, brought the barrel of the Colt across the man's face. Álvarez staggered back on one knee, the center of his face a sudden river of red. Through it, Fargo saw the mad snarl as the man shook his head and sprayed a shower of red in all directions.

Álvarez tried to raise the knife again, but Fargo drove the heavy Colt into his face with all the strength in his powerful shoulders. He heard the shattering sound of bone and gristle as the man's face fell in on itself. The Mexican swayed, stopped, swayed again, finally toppled backward, and Fargo heard the last few gurgled sounds as the man drowned in his own blood.

Fargo dropped to one knee for a moment, shook his head, wiped the Colt on the underbrush, and slowly pulled himself to his feet. He heard a distant rifle shot, another, but it was over, the shots only Álvarez's men firing at shadows as they fled. Those who were left to flee. He glanced down at the object spilling red on the ground. Juárez would have to get himself a new follower.

Turning away, Fargo reloaded the Colt as he made his way through the tall brush, saw the Ovaro, and whistled.

The horse trotted to him and he mounted and made his way back to the half-circle of rock. He saw three of the wranglers coming back with six of the Arabians, picking their way through the littered corpses of the attackers. Slim Staunton, Snyder, and Johnston, he saw as they neared. They had the horses tied together and well in hand.

"Tom and Karl Holst are bringing in four more," Slim said. "Dorrance and Jervis are chasing down half-a-dozen more. I expect we can round up the others, come morning. They'll roam, but not that far, not with their pals here with us. The horse is a herd animal."

"Anybody hurt?" Fargo asked.

"Not on our side," Slim answered, and Fargo gazed past him to see Tom Bessie and Holst returning with the four Arabians in tow. He waited for the men to reach him, saw Tom Bessie regard him with a mixture of amazement and admiration.

"You were right, Fargo. They didn't just come at us. They'd have poured lead into us if we'd all stayed bunched there and taken off with the Arabians. That's two in a row," Tom Bessie said. "That leaves only the Apache. You've something figured for them?"

"Not yet," Fargo said. "I'll sleep on it. Let's string these horses and get some shut-eye." He swung in beside the others and returned to the campsite. Another line was run, this time stringing the Arabians together and anchored at one end.

The others returned and bedrolls were brought out to stay. The camp turned silent and Fargo lay awake for a few moments longer on his blanket. "Only the Apache," he mused. Tom Bessie's words, not his. No one who knew the Indian would ever say *only* the Apache, even in passing. He let his eyes close, let his inner mind take over. Like an unseen ally, it shaped thoughts while he slept and let the conscious mind take credit, come the morning. He slept and knew the morning would come too soon.

Slim had been precisely right about the Arabians that had eluded the roundup after the attack. Fargo saw as soon as he woke a dark-brown mare moving like the wind across the flatland. He sat up, saw two more magnificent steeds prance into view, move in a wide circle, pause to sniff the air, retrace steps. He sat up and saw Tom Bessie, Slim, Johnston, and Karl Holst riding slowly, easily out across the flatland, lariats in hand. Snyder, Dorrance, and Jervis were already moving their horses in the other direction, starting to form a wide-mouthed pincers.

"They'll just figure to rope one or two," Art Silver said as he stayed with the tethered Arabians by the wall. "These aren't wild horses; they're just high-spirited, fiery critters. They take in one or two and the rest will come along."

Fargo rose, washed, and pulled on clothes as, with one eye, he watched the wranglers close their wide-mouthed pincers, adjust tactics as the Arabians galloped out of range, drifted back again. He had finished his second cup of coffee brewed in a heavy enamel pot over a small brush fire when he saw the spurt of movement, sudden twists and turns by horse and rider, and two of the Arabians were lassoed. He admired the smooth efficiency of men who knew their work as Tom Bessie led the way back and the last half-dozen Arabians followed along, skittishly but nonetheless following. The free horses pranced into the camp with the wranglers, and with a little backing and rearing let themselves be tied loosely with the others.

"We'll keep them strung for as long as we can," Tom

Bessie said. "Cut 'em loose when they get too restless. We could keep a pack of cow ponies strung for days and they'd just go along nice and peaceful, but not these critters."

"We go straight north," Fargo said as he climbed onto the Ovaro. "I'll ride on ahead some."

"Looking for anything special?" Holst asked.

"Anything that says Apache on it," he answered, and set off in a fast trot. The flatland began to rise into low hills, plenty of rock and red cedar, and he saw stands of gambel and blackjack oaks. He saw the profusion of Indian pony tracks also, and he halted at the base of the hills, dismounted to pick up a dusty brow band that lay on the ground. He brought it to his nose, sniffed, lowered it as his eyes swept the hills. He caught the flash of rock squirrels, a pair of white-tailed deer that moved slowly across his line of vision, and the perennial jackrabbits. He was still holding the brow band when the others rode up, the Arabians following. He saw Tom Bessie's eyes go to the piece of cloth.

"Apache," he said, and Tom's eyes questioned. "You smell the brow band of a Sioux or a Crow and you'll smell the buffalo grease and bear oil they put on their hair. The Apache uses sunflower-seed oil or an extract of creosote bush on his hair." He dropped the brow band and moved the Ovaro forward, started along the gentle rise of the hills. He halted at a spot with a brook and a good amount of clear land around it where they took time out to eat. The men consumed their food in silence and it was Slim Staunton who asked the question Fargo knew the others all wanted answered.

"You figure they've seen us, seen the Arabians?" he asked.

"They've seen. Plenty of fresh tracks around," Fargo said.

"Which means they'll be coming after the Arabians."

"You can count on it. Like putting a chicken in front of a fox," Fargo said.

"When?" one of the others questioned.

"Soon as they find the right spot. Their eyes are bugging out at the Arabians, even though they've probably never seen an Arabian before. But they know horses and they know that if the Arabians take off, they'll never be able to catch them with Indian ponies. They'll wait for a spot where they can strike and still keep the Arabians from taking off," Fargo said.

"Like a nice narrow pass," Tom Bessie muttered.

"Exactly." Fargo nodded.

"Then we stay out of narrow passes," Holst said.

"No way we can do that, going through these hills," Fargo said.

"So what do we do, just wait for them to hit us?" Tom Bessie asked. "We'll be sitting ducks."

"No, we don't do that. We give them what they want. We give them the Arabians," Fargo said. He felt the shock go through the others as they stared at him.

"I'll be damned. I never figured you'd take that out," Holst murmured. "Not that I'm objecting, if that's our way to stay alive."

"When we reach a pass, we'll stake out the Arabians and ride away from them. The Apache will know what we mean by it, a peace offering. We'll be giving them the Arabians for our scalps," Fargo said.

"That'll be about the truth of it," Bessie said.

"That's where knowing your Indians comes in. What we'll really be doing is taking what the Apache is and turning it against him," Fargo said, and saw frowns appear. "We could make a gesture like that with the Sioux, the Cheyenne, the Arapaho, almost any of the

Plains Indians. If they took the horses, it'd mean they'd agree to exchange and they'd honor that."

"But the Apache?" Holst asked.

"Their code is to make war, to kill the enemy, especially the white man. Their code is to use any way and any means to do that. They laugh at a code of honor that gets in the way of killing. The Apache respect power, strength, cunning, nothing else. This part of the country's full of the graves of people who didn't understand the Apache."

"What's that mean for us?" Tom Bessie asked.

"It means they'll take the Arabians we offer and then come after us, anyway," Fargo said. "They'll see us as just one more pack of stupid white fools and they'll come charging to lift our scalps, only this pack of damn fools will be waiting for them." He rose, let his eyes sweep the hills once more. "Let's move out. Waiting around won't make it any easier," he said. "The Arabians still in hand?"

"So far so good." Bessie nodded and Fargo climbed into the saddle and led the way up into the hills. He'd ridden perhaps another hour when he slowed, his gaze holding at the top of a rise to his left, and he heard a murmur from those riding behind him. A string of horsemen had appeared as if by magic, dark-bronze skins, many wearing sleeveless hide shirts. He counted twenty, all with long black hair that hung loose, kept in by brow bands. His eyes focused on the Apache at the center of the row of horsemen, bare-chested with a beaded brow band, a long bear-claw necklace hanging down to the middle of his chest. The very way he sat his pony proclaimed him as the leader.

"Just keep moving on," Fargo said to those behind him. "They want us to know they're there." He sent the Ovaro up along a gentle slope, and when he looked again, the Apaches had vanished.

"Jesus, they just disappeared," he heard Slim Staunton say. "I looked away and they were gone."

"They'll be back," Fargo said grimly.

His words proved themselves a little more than an hour later when, on the top line of a distant hill, the Apaches appeared again, sitting motionless on their horses. This time they stayed until Fargo and the others moved down the far side of another hill.

"What the hell are they doing?" Art Silver said. "They're giving me the creeps."

"That's the idea," Fargo said. "That's one of their weapons. Makes their targets come apart, softens them up. I've heard of wagon trains so unnerved they couldn't shoot straight by the time the Apache attacked. We'll just keep moving nice and easy."

He spurred the Ovaro forward, rode on ahead of the others, and halted at the top of the hill. The slope down was gentle enough, but it narrowed to the mouth of a pass. He waited, let the others come up, and saw the apprehension in their eyes as they espied the pass below.

"Move them down," he said. "I'm going through and see what's at the other end." He started down the hill toward the mouth of the pass, was halfway down when he spotted the Apache appear again, this time on his right, the top of a ridge looking down on the pass. He halted the Ovaro, let the Indians see him stare up at them, moved on after a moment. He rode into the pass at a trot, saw the sides rise up with good red-cedar cover and more than one pathway amid the trees.

He quickened his pace, saw the other end of the pass, and rode through. It widened some but not all that much. However, an immobile cascade of rocks rose up on both sides, like so many toys dumped by a giant. He halted, swung the Ovaro around, and went back through the pass, reached the mouth as Tom Bessie approached at the head of the Arabians, the other men stretched out on both sides of the horses. He spoke quietly to them as they went by him into the pass. "They're watching us. We reach the middle of the pass and dismount, stake out the Arabians, and ride on out," he said. "They can't see beyond the pass from up there. We'll be waiting when they come out after us."

He swung in behind the last of the men at the rear of the pack, dismounted as Tom Bessie halted at the center of the pass. Fargo glanced up to the ridge, saw the Apache peering down, unmoving as so many statues. The men drew the Arabians to the side, tethered the horses to a half-dozen trees, and Fargo made a point of looking up at the Indians again as he swung into the saddle.

"Ride easy," he muttered to the men as they started on through the remainder of the pass. He speeded up, took the lead as they reached the end of the pass. He slapped the pinto's rump as he cleared the end of the pass, and the horse went into a gallop. Fargo gestured to the rocks dumped on both sides of the area, raced almost to the last of the square stones, and swung the pinto in behind a cluster. Dismounting, he made certain the horse was hidden from sight, and he pulled the big Sharps rifle from the saddle holster, clambered up on the rocks. His glance swept the scene and he grunted in satisfaction. He saw nothing, the others already hidden in position.

He settled down against the rocks, waited, picked up the sounds of voices from in the pass. Though the Arabians were tethered, the Apache would leave three or four warriors to guard the horses, use a few minutes more to admire their prize. He raised the rifle in his hands, found a crevice in the rock perfect for resting the gun. He heard them before they came into sight, riding their unshod ponies hard on the witchgrass that covered the ground. The Apache charged out of the pass at a full gallop, the one with the bear-claw necklace in the lead. Fargo saw their eyes darting back and forth, peering ahead, intense, searching their quarry.

He waited for all of them to clear the end of the pass when the bare-chested leader raised his arm and pulled his pony to a halt. Fargo saw the frown on the Indian's face as the Apache suddenly realized something was wrong. Their quarry was nowhere in sight. Fargo aimed, fired, and saw the bear-claw necklace fly apart as the bullet caught the Indian full in the chest. The Apache catapulted backward from his pony as the air exploded with rifle fire. He saw four more of the Indians go down, started to draw a bead on another and cursed. They were Apache, and where others would have sought cover, presenting perfect targets as they raced for safety, the Apache raced their ponies forward, leaping up over the rocks, firing as they did, attacking instead of retreating. He saw three streaking toward him; one swerved to come around from the side and Fargo fired the rifle, hitting the one leaping head-on from his horse. He had to duck down as the second Apache's pony arched over his head, hooves almost brushing his hair. He whirled, and unable to bring the rifle around as the third Indian came at him from the side, he drew the Colt and got off one shot as the Apache leapt at him from his horse. He let himself slide down the smooth rock as the bullet slammed into the Indian in midair and the Apache crashed into the rock inches from his head.

Fargo landed at the base of the rock, rolled to see the Apache that had sailed over his head coming back again, his pony at a full gallop. Fargo raised the Colt and fired, but the Indian pulled back and the shot missed. Fargo swung the Colt, expecting the Apache to charge past him, but the Indian pulled his pony up sharply, spun and

Fargo had only time to glimpse the tomahawk hurtling through the air at him. He dropped facedown, and the tomahawk slammed into the rock a fraction of an inch over his head, showering slivers of stone down on him.

He pushed himself up and saw the Apache charging again, got the Colt up this time, and fired two shots. Both hit the Indian just below the breastbone. The pony skidded to a halt by itself to avoid running into the rocks and sent the Apache's body, trailing a stream of blood, sailing into the air. Fargo heard the man hit the ground as he reloaded the Colt and peered around the edge of a rock. Apaches lay on the ground, littered forms, a half-dozen draped across the rocks, and he grabbed for the Sharps as he saw one Indian vaulting onto a pony, starting to race back into the pass. He fired and the Apache twisted on the pony's back, fell forward over the animal's withers, finally toppled to the ground as the pony raced on.

Fargo rose, spun, leapt onto the Ovaro, and saw Karl Holst stand up over a rock, Tom Bessie pulling himself up alongside him. Holst had a gash across his temple, Bessie a cut alongside his jaw. Fargo raced the Ovaro by the two wranglers and into the pass and saw the Arabians still tethered to the trees; an Apache had a skinning knife in his hand trying to sever the ropes. The Indian turned as he heard Fargo racing toward him, ran past the Arabians, and leapt onto his pony. He was a small form low over the horse's back as he streaked away, and Fargo lowered the rifle. The Apache kept going and Fargo saw a second Indian swing out from the side of the pass and race on beside him. They had fought with savage abandon and had lost. To flee was no disgrace. That was for those burdened with strange codes. Losing was only the recognition of power.

Fargo wheeled the Ovaro around and rode back out of

the pass to see Dorrance and Jervis on the ground, Slim and Holst carrying the limp, still form of Art Silver from behind a pair of rocks. He dismounted and walked forward. Dorrance's eyes were open, pain in his face. "Leg's broken. Goddamn tomahawk," Tom Bessie said. "We can make a splint that'll hold him till we get him to a doc."

Fargo nodded, his gaze going to Jervis. The hole in the man's chest made questions unnecessary. "Jervis and Art Silver," he said. "Who else?"

"Nobody. I think we'll all be carrying some scars, but nothing we can't handle," Bessie said.

"Get the splint ready. Three of you come with me and fetch the Arabians," Fargo said.

Holst and two of the others came along and the afternoon wore down as Fargo raised his arm, started forward once again. Dorrance rode strapped to the saddle, his left leg stretched out stiff in the splint, and Fargo moved slowly, his own weariness heavy on him. They managed to cover enough ground to find a stream and a stand of red cedars alongside it as dark descended. No one felt like eating, and bedrolls came out quickly. They'd fashioned proper graves back on the hillside for Jervis and Art Silver, and Fargo stretched out, his face grim.

"Wasn't your fault," Tom Bessie said, reading his thoughts. "Weren't for you we'd all be back there dead." He lay back on his blanket. "You got us past all of them, the French, that crazy Mexican, and now the Apache. Nothing now but some good hard trail riding. The worst is over."

He was right, Fargo murmured silently. They'd come through. Why did he still feel a strange uneasiness? Maybe he'd just been too wound up for too long. A good night's sleep and a new day would push it all away, he told himself. He closed his eyes, welcomed the sleep that swept over him at once.

He slept heavily and it was the soft dawn wind that woke him. Or he thought it was the soft dawn wind, a gentle puff of air across his face. He opened his eyes, pushed himself onto one elbow, blinked in the gray dawn light. He saw long, jet hair first, then a delicately modeled, lovely face, only inches away from his. He saw lovely lips come together, blow another soft, gentle puff of air into his face. He blinked again, unsure if he were dreaming, and then he saw the long-barreled Whitneyville Colt in front of his face. He was dreaming, he told himself. But the gun barrel was pushed into his forehead, cold and hard. He was not dreaming.

"What in hell?" he breathed, heard Tom Bessie turn on his bedroll nearby.

"I'll take that," Isabel whispered, reached out, and took the Colt from the holster beside him, pushed it into her waist. She smiled and he saw sadness and coldness mixed together.

He found his voice. "What the hell are you doing here?" he growled.

She pushed back from her knees, stood up, and he saw Tom Bessie open his eyes, frown. Holst woke a few feet away, blinked. Isabel stepped quickly, came up behind him, and Fargo felt the barrel against his temple.

"Goddammit, what are you doing here?" he growled again, louder this time.

"I've come for my Arabians," she said softly.

He started to turn, but the gun pressed harder into his temple. "No, please, don't do anything we'll both be sorry for," she said.

"You out of your goddamn head?" He frowned, saw the others waking, sitting up, frowning.

168

"No one moves. I'm not experienced at this sort of thing. This gun could go off," Isabel said.

"Take that damn gun away from my head," Fargo said. He heard her whistle, a sudden, sharp sound, and he stared in disbelief as the figures came into view, six men on horseback, moving down the slope from the red cedars. All armed, he saw, two with guns out. Most wore the flat-brimmed *poblanos*, one a stetson, all were Mexicans, hard-faced men with mustaches, three with long sideburns. They rode their horses among Fargo's still-sleepy wranglers, gestured with their hands, quick, imperative gestures that were unmistakable. Tom Bessie handed his gun over first, Holst next, and the others followed.

"That knife in the calf holster, Fargo," Isabel said almost sweetly.

He reached down, drew the thin blade out, and she took it, tossed it to the man with the stetson. She stepped back and Fargo turned to see that the black eyes had almost grown soft as she met his angry stare. "I'm sorry. I told you I couldn't let you take the Arabians. I tried not to have it come to this," she said.

He let his lips purse, remembered the words that had stabbed at him, "I'm trying to find a way out of this."

"You'd prepared long ago," he said.

"As soon as my father made the deal with Bill Alderson, when I realized I couldn't make him change his mind," she said. "I hired these men, paid them to wait. I hoped you wouldn't go through with it, but when you did, I called them in."

"What took you so long getting here?" he asked, not without an edge of bitterness in his voice.

He saw pain flood her face for a moment. "Things," she answered. "Things." She paused, lost in thought for another second, and shook herself back to the moment.

"It wasn't hard to follow your trail," she said. "I was afraid I'd be too late each time, but you kept winning, going on."

"A habit of mine. Aren't you proud of me?" he tossed at her with angry sarcasm.

She smiled and he hated the sweet loveliness of her lips. "Yes, strangely enough," she said softly, erased the smile from her face, and he heard harshness come into her voice. "But it's over now," she said and tossed commands in Spanish at the six men, who then rounded up every horse. Isabel reached out and took the reins of the Ovaro. "I think Sonora is the next town. It will be a long walk, but you'll make it," she said.

"One of my men has a splint on his leg," Fargo protested.

"Carry him," she snapped. She started off leading the Ovaro, and one of her men brought her horse to her. She swung onto the saddle as Fargo shouted at her.

"Goddammit, Isabel, you can't leave us here without a damn horse," he said.

"You'll make it to Sonora, I'm sure," she said.

"Bitch," he yelled.

Her eyes met his anger and he saw the sadness in the black orbs again. "Yes, perhaps," she said thoughtfully. She turned the horse, snapped orders again in Spanish, and he watched in furious frustration as the six men followed her, the Arabians in tow. She disappeared down the slope, behind a line of the red cedars, and he saw Tom Bessie and the others staring at him.

"Don't bother explaining. We can put enough of it together," Tom said. "Whoever she is, she's one hell of a piece of woman."

"Isabel Teresa Concepción Consaldo-López," Fargo bit out. "That's who she is, and I didn't read her right, goddammit."

"I'm going to start walking," Tom Bessie said.

"I'm going after her," Fargo said.

"On foot?" The man frowned.

"I'll keep up," Fargo said, aware that the man had no knowledge of his ways. "She's got this damn thing about those Arabians and she's going to lose it all, anyway."

"You're crazy, Fargo. But good luck," Bessie said.

"You all start walking. You'll be riding again soon," Fargo said. He moved forward, pulled on clothes, broke into a trot first, disappeared into the trees, and let his long, powerful legs stretch out. When he started downhill, he was in a long, crouched, loping gait, every part of his body coordinated, the ground-eating gait that, not unlike a gray wolf, he could maintain with seeming tirelessness. But he wouldn't need to maintain it for long, he was certain. He had seen the way the six men had looked at the Arabians.

He moved through the cedars, up the long slopes, down the other sides, following the trail with ease. He almost smiled as he espied the horses halted near the edge of a stand of black walnut. He veered, made his way into the trees, moved through the stand with the silence of a wolf. He neared the horses, saw Isabel's face icy with rage. "You have no honor, none of you," he heard her say.

The six men were still on foot, the horses nearby. The one with the stetson shrugged. "Honor brings no money. The Arabians will bring a small fortune," he said. "One takes opportunity when one finds it. *Adiós, señorita.*"

Fargo poised at the edge of the trees. The man had his Colt as well as his throwing knife, he saw. One of the six had wandered closer to the trees, his gaze admiring the Arabians. He had a Walker Colt in his holster. Fargo rose on the balls of his feet. He'd have but one chance. It had to be fast and vicious. There was no other way. He gath-

171

ered himself, tightened powerful thigh muscles. When he shot from the edge of the trees, he was as a cougar springing on its prey. He hurtled into the man, his hand yanking the gun from his holster as he sent the figure sprawling. He hit the ground, rolled, saw the others whirl, surprise on their faces. They were close together, almost in a knot. Fargo fired from half on his back, a furious volley of shots. The five men toppled in all directions, not unlike tenpins in a bowling alley. Fargo swung the gun at the sixth man, saw he was running for his life, half-falling, sobbing in terror.

Fargo lowered the gun, got to his feet. He walked to the lifeless form of the man in the stetson, retrieved his Colt and his knife, finally turned to Isabel. Her eyes were wide with surprise. "You know something?" he bit out. "You might be stupid, but you are beautiful."

"I trusted them. I didn't think they'd turn on me," she said.

"You didn't think," he rasped.

She stepped forward, came close to him. "You don't understand. I had to come after the Arabians. They were all I had left," she said, and his eyes frowned at her. "Before Álvarez came after you, he hit the ranch with all his men. He burned the place to the ground. The Arabians that were there ran off."

"Don Miguel, Alfredo?" Fargo asked.

"Killed," she said. "I would have been, too, but I wasn't there. Álvarez left when the French came after they saw the flames. I came back later that night." She leaned her head against his chest. "Nothing worked right, nothing," she half-sobbed. "Except you. You came after me again. Or maybe only the Arabians this time."

"Both of you," he said. "Get your damn horse. I want to get to the men before they've walked too far, and you're coming with me, all the way."

"All the way?" she frowned.

"You heard me. You've nothing left in Mexico now. You have property, interests, but you can attend to those later. You're going to Bill Alderson. You'll work for him. He'll be happy as all hell to have you there running his breeding program. You've got it all in your head. You can see to it that it goes on the way you want it to."

Her eyes were wide. "He would do that, your Señor Alderson? He would let me work with him?"

"I told you, he'll be happy as all hell, probably give me a bonus for bringing you," Fargo said.

She lifted her arms around his neck and her lips pressed hard against his. "And you will stay?" she asked.

"For a while," he said.

"You will work for Señor Alderson?" she asked.

"Not exactly. I figure to be offering my own stud service," he said.

Her lips edged a little smile, smug and sly at once. "Yes, you will indeed. Indeed," she murmured as her lips pressed his again.

Fire and ice, he mused silently. Whoever said they didn't mix?

LOOKING FORWARD

The following is the opening section
from the next novel in the exciting
Trailsman series from Signet:

THE TRAILSMAN #32
APACHE GOLD

---

*Gold City, deep in Arizona territory,
where Apache gold and miners'
blood are mingling . . .*

SKYE FARGO sat up, suddenly alert.

"What's the matter, honey?" the buxom blonde asked, lifting her head and staring up at him. "There ain't no need for you to stop now. You doin' just great."

"Downstairs. That racket. A chair breaking, I think."

Then came the sound of heavy, running feet.

Moving with the speed and grace of a mountain cat, Fargo left the bed and hurried to the window. Peering down, he saw men running from the saloon, others rushing toward it. A shoot-out was coming, maybe. Fargo didn't like that. The floor in this place offered as little protection as the walls.

As he pulled away from the window, Fargo's lean, hawk-like face crinkled into a devilish grin. Sometimes trouble had a way of clearing his head—like a drink of cold, fresh, spring water.

"There's trouble brewing downstairs," he told the blonde. "I'll be right back."

Disappointment clouded her face as she sat up and watched him, her eyes feasting on his nakedness.

"Honey," she said, "let them fight. What's that got to do with us?"

"If they start shooting down there, we're liable to catch a stray slug. Or a lamp could overturn and start a fire." He winked at her. "I was planning on spending the night here with you, remember?"

A shade over six feet tall, Skye Fargo was big enough to hunt bears with a switch. As he plucked his buckskin pants off the chair and got ready to step into them, a bear-claw scar in the shape of a half moon became visible on his forearm, while the muscles on his massive shoulders and torso stood out like mole tunnels. His unruly black hair—the color of a raven's wing—hung almost to his shoulders.

Buttoning up his fly, Fargo had a momentary problem with a portion of his anatomy that refused to believe he was not staying in bed with the blonde. Watching him from the bed, the blond was having trouble with the idea also.

"See how that big feller don't want to go down, honey," she pouted. "Why don't you just stay up here with me?"

Grinning, Fargo turned and strode back to her. Sweeping up one ample breast in his big palm, he kissed the nipple. "I won't be goin' far, Rose. I promise you. When I get back, you'll be glad I went. You stay right where you are. Hear?"

The blonde nodded doubtfully and slid down under the sheet, her eyes watching him curiously as he slipped out the door.

From the stairway's first floor landing, Fargo paused and looked down at the crowded bar. He had guessed right. There was trouble, all right. A chair was overturned and in the center of the room two men were slowly circling each other. Around them, forming a ring of spectators, stood the saloon's patrons, their jaws slack, their eyes filled with a blood lust. Like a wolf pack circling a crippled doe, they were waiting for the kill.

Fargo had just ridden into Gold City only a few days before, but already he knew the two men squaring off. The smaller of the two was Rex Barry, a Wells, Fargo shotgun messenger. White-haired and in his fifties, he was shorter by a foot than the other one. In a worn, leather holster he carried an ancient Colt. Fargo had shared a couple of drinks with him earlier in the day and liked him.

The other one was Slade Kingston, a gambler recently arrived from a Mississippi steamboat. Fargo had disliked him almost from the first. And he was almost certain Slade had not dealt every card from the top of the deck while playing poker with Fargo that afternoon. But Fargo had had other irons in the fire at the time and had not challenged him.

Fargo saw clearly what must have just happened. Rex Barry had accused the gambler of cheating and now Slade was bullying him into a gunfight that could have only one outcome. The white-haired shotgun messenger was no gunfighter.

Fargo started down the stairs.

He had almost reached the saloon floor when the two men stopped circling each other and Slade Kingston's sharp, grating voice boomed out in the hushed saloon.

"You heard me, Barry! I expect an apology!"

"I slapped you 'cause you deserved it, Slade," Barry

said, edging back. "You called me a fool and a poor loser."

Slade's eyebrows went up slightly. "And you implied I hadn't been playing fairly."

"If the shoe fits."

"You are scum, sir. I demand satisfaction."

"You won't get any apology from me," Barry replied stoutly.

Slade dropped his hand to the grips of his gleaming, pearl-handled Colt .45. The ring of spectators pushed back quickly.

"You're wearing a gun, Barry," Slade said. "I expect you'd better get ready to use it."

"You can't make me draw, Slade!"

Fargo was not armed, and before he could do anything, Slade drew his Colt. It was a fast draw, lightning fast.

Barry flung both hands up over his head.

"No, Slade," the man cried. "I told you. I won't draw!"

Slade appeared ready to shoot anyway, the muzzle of his Colt aimed at Barry's midsection. Barry began to sweat, but he did not crawl.

Abruptly, Slade lowered his Colt, then strode over to Barry and slammed the old man brutally on the side of the head. Barry's hat went flying as he toppled like a tree, his head knocking a cuspidor to one side as it crunched into the floor. Blood oozed thickly from a deep gash over the old man's temple.

Slade stepped back, then kicked Barry viciously in the side. Barry groaned slightly and raised a forearm in a feeble attempt to ward off the next blow.

It never came.

Fargo had reached Slade Kingston by that time. He caught Slade's right arm and spun him around. Slade was a dandy, his full head of dark hair well groomed, his mustache closely trimmed. He was wearing a black frock coat and tan trousers that followed closely the line of his calves. His boots were highly polished.

"Back off, Slade!" Fargo told him.

Kingston pulled himself angrily out of Fargo's grasp. "This isn't your affair," he said, his dark eyes snapping angrily.

"I just dealt myself in."

"You're a fool then."

"You calling me a fool, are you? Now *I* want satisfaction."

Kingston glanced contemptuously down at Fargo's waist. "You're not armed."

"Sure, I am," Fargo said, holding up his two fists.

"I am a gentleman, sir. It is not my practice to brawl with half-naked louts."

"I see. You just cheat at cards and beat up old men. Is that it?"

Kingston's cruelly handsome face went pale. Fargo smiled, enjoying Slade's discomfiture. "Later, Fargo." the gambler managed, turning his back on Fargo and striding over to the bar. "Later. You'll get your turn. I promise you."

"Sure, Slade. But I'm warning you. The next time you play cards with me, you'd better keep both hands on the table—and your sleeves empty."

At this second, deliberate insult, the gambler's shoulders stiffened. He placed both hands palm down on the top of the bar to steady himself, then glanced in the mirror behind the bar as he addressed Fargo.

"I know what your intentions are," he said, "but I will not be provoked!"

Fargo walked up behind Slade, grabbed him by the

shoulder, and spun him around. Then he slapped him—
hard. Tears of rage flooded Slade's eyes. This time Slade
went for his gun, but Fargo caught his right wrist and
twisted. Gasping, Slade went down on one knee. Fargo
lifted the gun from Slade's holster and flung it across the
room. Then he hauled Slade to his feet, turned him
roughly, and with a powerful kick sent him windmilling
out through the batwing doors. From outside the saloon,
the sharp crack of a hitch-rail snapping under Slade's
weight was followed by that of startled horses whinnying
in surprise, then rearing and clattering away from the
front of the saloon.

Fargo turned around then and walked over to the still
unconscious Rex Barry. He picked Barry up and carried
him in his arms over to a faro table. The entire right side
of the shotgun messenger's face was encased in a dark
shell of coagulating blood. Fargo thought there was a
good chance the old man's skull had been fractured.

Putting Barry down gently on the faro table, Fargo
turned to those men crowding around.

"Get a doctor!"

Someone in the rear of the crowd turned and bolted
from the saloon. By this time, the saloon was filled with
excited patrons, who now crowded around Fargo, their
faces beaming, their hands reaching out to shake his
hand or slap him on the back.

Pulling back from the crowd, he looked around into
their faces and said quietly, "Not a single one of you men
stepped forward to help this man."

"It wasn't our fight."

"Yeah!" said another. "He accused Kingston of
cheating."

"You know he does. Even so, you all just stood around
gaping."

"That ain't fair, mister."

"How fair was it when Slade clubbed Barry to the ground?"

To that there was only a sullen, cowed silence.

Those standing closest to Fargo glanced uneasily at each other and took a step back. The men behind them moved back also, avoiding Fargo's quietly accusing eyes as they did so. Others moistened their lips to say something, then thought better of it. Some hurried from the saloon, others hunched up to the bar like whipped children.

Abruptly, the fellow who had gone for the doctor returned with him. The doctor was a tall, cadaverous-looking fellow who hurried over to the faro table and immediately bent to examine Barry.

After a swift examination, the doctor glanced up at Fargo.

"Is he going to be all right?" Fargo asked the doctor.

"He has a mild concussion—but it could get worse if he doesn't keep himself quiet. I'll need help to move him to his room."

Fargo's eyes caught the eyes of two husky-looking men sitting at a nearby table. One glance was all that was needed. The two men got hastily to their feet, and under the doctor's direction, helped carry the still unconscious shotgun messenger from the saloon.

That accomplished, Fargo took a deep breath. Then he went over to the bar, purchased a bottle of whiskey and started back up the stairs to Rose.

When he entered her room a moment later and locked the door behind him, she glanced over at him somewhat apprehensively. He smiled as he put the bottle on the floor near the bed and swiftly peeled off his britches and climbed into bed beside her. Sighing in relief, she spread herself happily to receive him. He entered her lush warmth easily, plunging deep. She gasped in delight and flung her arms around his neck as she took all of him.

"Go deeper!" she gasped.

"How's that?"

"Deeper!"

He obliged.

"Mmmm! Oh, yes, yes!"

A moment later Rose screamed and flung her arms around his neck. But he didn't let up. He just kept driving.

The next morning Rose and he were having breakfast across the street in Ma Boyle's restaurant when a tall, bluff fellow dressed in a well-tailored dark suit strode into the place. He was obviously looking for someone, and when he spotted Fargo, he headed immediately for his table. Fargo knew him as Tim Bridger, the Wells, Fargo agent in Gold City.

"Sit down," said Fargo. "Join us."

"I already had breakfast, Fargo," Bridger said. His voice was unpleasantly officious. And he refused even to acknowledge Rose's presence at the table. "But maybe I'll join you in coffee."

"Suit yourself."

After the waitress came over and took his order for coffee, Tim cleared his throat. "Rex is still hurt pretty bad, Fargo," he said. "But the doc says he'll be all right if he takes a nice, long rest."

Fargo nodded. He had figured as much.

"I came over to ask if you'd do me a favor," Bridger said.

Fargo glanced up from his eggs and bacon, a gleam in

his lake-blue eyes. "I already did my good deed for the week."

"I know that, Fargo, and we all appreciate your standing up to Slade Kingston like that. But now we got a problem."

"I'm listenin'."

"We need a man to ride shotgun."

Fargo considered. He did not wish to appear anxious, but it had immediately occurred to him that this might fit quite nicely into his plans. He had come to Arizona because he had heard of the Bart Mullin gang, which had been preying on this particular stage route for the past six months. A description of a member of the gang matched the description of one of the men Fargo was searching for—one of the men who had killed his father, a famous Wells, Fargo stage driver in his own right.

"What's the pay?" Fargo asked cautiously.

"On this trip?"

Fargo nodded.

"Five dollars a day."

"That's pretty steep, ain't it? You expecting a war to break out?"

"There have been several holdups in the past month. Wells, Fargo is determined to protect its coaches, and you seem to be a man capable of giving it that protection."

"I'll need a Greener."

"You can use Rex's. He sure as hell won't be needing it for a while."

"When's the stage pulling out?"

"In an hour."

"That doesn't give me much time."

Bridger shrugged.

Rose spoke up then. "Word around town is there's a big gold shipment going out today."

Bridger looked at Rose for the first time. It was obvious he did not approve of her, or her profession—at least not while he was sober. "Fool talk," he snapped at her. "The same talk that's been going around for weeks."

"Then there's nothing of any value being shipped today?" Fargo asked.

"I didn't say that. There's always valuables, on every run. That's why we have a strong box."

Fargo nodded, studying Bridger's face—and eyes—intently. He didn't like the evasiveness he sensed in them.

"Well?" Bridger asked, "will you take the job?"

"Sure. At five dollars a day, how can I go wrong?"

Bridger stood up. "Fine. I'll tell Bill Gifford. He'll be the Jehu on this run."

Fargo nodded. As Bridger turned and started from the restaurant, Fargo got to his feet.

"Just a minute, Bridger!" he said softly.

Bridger pulled up and swung around, a frown on his face.

"What do you want, Fargo?" Bridger asked.

Fargo smiled. "You have lousy manners, Bridger. You forgot to greet my breakfast guest when you sat down, then you forgot to bid her good day when you left. I'm sure it was just an oversight."

Bridger swallowed angrily, but the cold light in Fargo's eyes restrained him. He doffed his hat, bowed politely to Rose, and said, "Good day, ma'am."

Rose smiled and inclined her head slightly.

Swinging back around angrily, Bridger strode from the restaurant.

Fargo took his Ovaro from the town's livery stable and rode him over to the Wells, Fargo horse barn and told the hostler, Sim Tompkins, that if he didn't take good care of him, Fargo would force feed him a bucket full of oats—without water—when he got back. Fargo grinned when he said this, but Tompkins understood that Fargo was most anxious to see to it that his horse was well taken care of while he was on this run. Tompkins promised Fargo that he could rest easy.

"He's a damn pretty Ovaro," Tompkins commented appreciatively. "Nicest piece of horseflesh I've seen in a long time. Be a pleasure to groom him. He'll be a mite fat and sassy by the time you get back, though. Want me to breeze him out once in a while?"

"I'd appreciate it," said Fargo. "Just go easy on him. You won't need rowels."

"I can see that."

Fargo left the man and carried his gear over to the waiting stagecoach. The six-horse team had already been backed into the traces and two stable boys were now busy harnessing up the team. Fargo climbed up into the box and stowed his personal gear on the storage rack on top of the coach. Then he clambered down to get the Greener waiting for him in the express office. As he mounted the steps to the office, he encountered the driver just coming out.

"What's going out this morning?" Fargo asked him.

"A whiskey drummer, a mail sack, and a strongbox."

"What's in the strong box?"

Bill Gifford sent a black dart of tobacco juice out of the corner of his mouth. "Valuables."

"That's not much help, Bill."

"There ain't no gold in it, if that's what you're thinkin'."

With a shrug, Fargo moved past the driver into the office and took down Barry's Greener from the rack. He broke it to check it out, then looked up at Bridger to ask for shells. The big man was way ahead of him. Without a word, he handed Fargo a small box of shells.

."Thanks, Bridger," Fargo said.

The Wells, Fargo agent did not bother to respond. Fargo guessed he was still seething inwardly from that scene earlier in the restaurant when he had been forced to bid Rose a polite goodbye.

Fargo smiled to himself and walked back outside to look over the coach. He was impressed. The body was painted a bright red. The leather of the front and rear boots was black and gleaming, the wheel's yellow spokes and rims shining from a recent waxing. The brake shoes looked hardly worn, in fact.

Cass Terhune, a Wells, Fargo clerk whom Fargo had met earlier that morning stepped up onto the porch and paused beside Fargo, admiring with him the bright new stagecoach.

"She's a beauty, ain't she," said Cass.

"Sure is."

"We spent all night getting her ready."

"It looks it."

"Good luck, Mr. Fargo," Cass said, his long face suddenly creasing in a grin. "I sure admire you for helping out Rex yesterday."

"Why, thank you, Cass."

With a nod, Fargo left the clerk, crossed the yard to the stage and clambered up beside Bill Gifford.

"So we're breaking in a new coach, are we?"

"Yep," the driver said proudly. "This is its first run. So let's make sure nothin' bad happens to it."

Fargo nodded and looked down to inspect the Greener. It was well-oiled and appeared to be in excellent shape. It did not look as if Rex Barry had ever fired it in anger. This did not lull Fargo, however. Like Rose, he had heard the talk in town about a gold shipment. The way the story went, fear that Bart Mullin's gang would rob the assay office had prompted Wells, Fargo headquarters in San Francisco to direct Bridger to ship out whatever gold ingots they were storing by the earliest possible stage.

Bill Gifford spat a long rope of tobacco juice out of his mouth. He was impatient.

"What are we waiting for?" Fargo asked.

"The sheriff. He's personally escorting a friend of his to the stage."

At that moment Sheriff Sands appeared, hauling a whiskey drummer down the boardwalk toward the express office. The drummer was walking unsteadily and the sheriff was doing what he could to keep the man upright. The drummer, his white shirt stained and his collar hanging by one button, lost his derby hat twice as the sheriff helped him along. Reaching the coach, the sheriff boosted the inebriated salesman through the door, then looked up at Gifford and Fargo.

The sheriff was a blockily-built man with broad, beetling brows and features that seemed squeezed together. At the moment his small dark eyes gleamed with surprising malevolence.

"You two take good care of my friend here," he warned them. "I don't want nothing to happen to him."

"Why don't you ride along?" suggested Fargo, "seein' you're that concerned."

"Do I know you?"

"Name's Fargo, Skye Fargo."

"You're the one faced down Slade Kingston yesterday."

"That's right," said Bill Gifford, "while you was out carousin' with this here whiskey drummer."

"Now, just a minute there!"

Ignoring the sheriff's angry response, Gifford fitted the ribbons into his thick, gnarled fingers. "Stand back, sheriff," he cried. "We got a run to make!"

Gifford took his foot off the brake and cursed with full-throated eloquence at his team. Then he sent his whip cracking over the six gleaming backs. The sheriff stepped hastily back as the six powerful horses broke into a trot. Rocking on its leather thoroughbraces, the stage rolled out of town toward a brightening morning sky. It was going to be another hot one, Fargo realized.

Three hours later, the sun was a blazing ingot burning a hole in the back of his neck. Both men were covered from heat to foot with alkali dust, their eyes peering through slitted lids at a cruel, brass-yellow world of sun-blasted rock and desert. There had been no peep out of their single passenger since leaving Gold City, and neither one of them had bothered to check on the fellow. Since he was the only passenger, he was probably stretched out on one of the benches, oblivious to the world he was passing through as he slept off his drunk.

Fargo himself was thinking back on Gold City. He was glad to be putting the raw town behind him—though he would certainly miss Rose.

Gold City he had found to be a typical boom town, feeding on the recently discovered gold being panned in the streams nearby. There was talk of gold further into the mountains, but the Apaches had so far kept most prospectors from advancing into them. The result was a town swarming with anxious, angry prospectors, lounging on the boardwalks or swilling booze in the saloons, all of them champing at the bit to get into those golden mountains, as they were called.

Gifford cleared his throat. Fargo looked at him.

"Just thought you ought to know somethin'," he said.

"Go ahead," Fargo shouted above the rattle of the coach.

"Before we left Gold City I got word that Shriber's station was hit by Apaches."

"When?"

"Late yesterday."

"How bad was it?"

"All that's left is a chimney and some pretty poor looking corpses that used to work for Wells, Fargo. Naratena's renegades, more'n likely."

"Naratena? Who's he?"

"Apache war chief. He's been doing his best to keep the prospectors out of these mountains. And so far, he's been real successful."

"What's he got against stagecoaches?"

"That's what I can't rightly understand. Up until now he's never touched a single Wells, Fargo coach or way-station."

Abruptly, the stage slammed down into a twisting grade that led between two towering rock pillars. After they rocked on through them, almost at once the horses began a straining upward climb that had Bill flicking the ribbons constantly. Higher and higher the stage climbed into the rocky fastness. As he glanced around, Fargo found growing within him a grudging admiration for the rugged, wild beauty of this fantastic land of towering monuments, twisting canyons, and walls of sheer, polished rock.

This particular badland had been labeled the Devil's Playground. Fargo realized how apt the name was as he peered about him at the ponderous, hunched creatures of rock that met his gaze on all sides. From the look of their twisted, gargoyle-like shapes, they reminded Fargo of lost souls frozen into attitudes of eternal torment.

"Keep your eyes peeled," Bill grumbled, breaking into Fargo's thoughts. "We're comin' into Apache country now."

They came to a sudden downgrade, and Bill slammed his booted foot onto the brake, keeping it there. At the bottom of the grade, he saw that a sudden downpour had gouged a deep cut cross the stage road's twin ruts. He shifted the Greener in his lap as the stage rocked on toward it. Bill hunched forward almost eagerly as he tightened his grips on the reins.

"Steady there!" he cried to his horse. "Keep a goin', damn you!"

The six horses plunged down the near side of the wash. The stage rocked forward dangerously as it plunged crazily down over the cut's rim. With a roar the wheels slammed into the wash's gravel bed. Pebbles and good-sized stones went flying. The coach skittered to one side, and for a moment Fargo was certain it was going to tip over onto its side. But the horses did not falter as Bill shouted to the leaders and urged them on with a scalding mixture of endearments and blasphemies.

Up the far side of the wash the horses lunged, their powerful muscles bunching, their hooves sending soft clods of dirt flying. They gained the rim, and a second later—rocking dangerously—the stage was pulled out of the wash and lunged after them, swaying treacherously.

As Bill hauled back on the reins and settled the horses into a more leisurely pace, he turned to Fargo with a pleased grin, his right cheek bulging with his chaw. Then he spat out a long, black stream of tobacco juice.

"This here's a great team," he shouted above the roar of the coach. "I picked out each horse myself."

Fargo started to reply, but Bill's right cheekbone vanished. With it went Bill's eye and a portion of his jaw. As the report from the rifle that killed Bill echoed above the rattle of the stage, Bill dropped the reins and tumbled back off the box.

Fargo did not hear the second rifle shot. But he saw a portion of the seat beside him disintegrate as the slug slammed into it. By this time the horses were bolting, the reins having fallen down among the traces. The stage picked up speed precipitously and began to rock wildly along. Another slug whined off the iron baggage rack. The horses were now galloping full out.

As Fargo tried to climb down onto the traces to grab the reins, the stage's right wheel struck a boulder. The entire coach lifted. Fargo tried to reach back and grab the box, but he missed it by inches and went peeling back off the plunging stagecoach. He struck the hard-packed ground a jolting blow, landing on his shoulders. But it was the back of his head that absorbed most of the shock.

Lights exploded deep within his skull, and that was all he remembered.

Naratena, the Apache chieftain, had seen it all.

Cradling a gleaming rifle in his arm, he stood erect on the ledge high overhead, watching impassively as first the stage driver, then the shotgun messenger toppled from the stage.

The squat, powerfully built chief was dressed in a buckskin shirt and breechclout. A clean white headband kept his thick, lustrous black hair in place, and on his feet he wore the traditional Apache mocassins, the *n-deh b'keh*, a thigh-length, thick-soled footgear that enabled the Apache warrior to cover 70 miles a day on foot over this cruel and unrelenting ground.

Naratena's face was typical of the Mescalaro Apache—broad and rather flat, except for his dark-blue eyes and sharply prominent nose, legacies of a fierce Spanish grandmother whose voice had always carried weight in tribal council.

Behind Naratena, on a ledge about six feet lower, a line of silent warriors waited. All but two of them carried bright new rifles. The remaining two, the youngest, carried the traditional weapons of the Apache—a rawhide sling, elmwood bow and deerskin case, and the nine-foot long war lances tipped with steel blades. The elmwood bows had a lethal range of 100 yards and their slings were capable of hurling stones at least fifty yards farther. All eighteen of the warriors watched their chief with eager, impatient eyes—like hounds straining on their leashes.

Naratena went down suddenly on one knee and, using his rifle for support, leaned far out over the ledge to see more clearly who had been firing at the stagecoach. What he saw caused him to grunt softly. Then, below him on the stage trail, the stagecoach struck a boulder, careened wildly, and slammed over onto its side, disintegrating as it struck the ground. The horses, terrified, continued on, dragging their traces after them.

Naratena got back up onto his feet, turned to his braves and waved them off the ledge. Then he followed after them swiftly, silently, his Apache moccasins leaving no trace on the hot, searing stone.

JOIN THE *TRAILSMAN* READERS' PANEL

Help us bring you more of the books you like by filling out this survey and mailing it in today.

1. Book title:_____

Book #:_____

2. Using the scale below how would you rate this book on the following features.

Poor		Not so Good			O.K.			Good		Excellent
0	1	2	3	4	5	6	7	8	9	10

Rating

Overall opinion of book . . . . _____
Plot/Story . . . . _____
Setting/Location . . . . _____
Writing Style . . . . _____
Character Development . . . . _____
Conclusion/Ending . . . . _____
Scene on Front Cover . . . . _____

3. On average about how many western books do you buy for yourself each month?_____

4. How would you classify yourself as a reader of westerns?
I am a ( ) light ( ) medium ( ) heavy reader.

5. What is your education?
( ) High School (or less)   ( ) 4 yrs. college
( ) 2 yrs. college   ( ) Post Graduate

6. Age_____   **7.** Sex: ( ) Male ( ) Female

Please Print Name_____

Address_____

City_____State_____Zip_____

Phone # (   )_____

Thank you. Please send to New American Library, Research Dept, 1633 Broadway, New York, NY 10019.